The Country Knight

Book 1 of the Rowanark Tournament Series

George Kayde

CR&C Studios
Toronto, Ontario

George Kayde
CR&C Studios
Unit 1021
20 Minowan Miikan Lane
Toronto, Ontario M6J 0E5
www.georgekayde.com

Publisher's Note: This is a work of fiction. Names, characters, places, and incidents are a product of the author's imagination. Locales and public names are sometimes used for atmospheric purposes. Any resemblance to actual people, living or dead, or to businesses, companies, events, institutions, or locales is completely coincidental.

Ordering Information:
Quantity sales. Special discounts are available on quantity purchases by corporations, associations, and others. For details, contact the "Special Sales Department" at the address above.

The Country Knight / George Kayde — 1st ed.

Get Your Free Starter Library!

Sign up for the no-spam Reader's List and get **TWO** free books, and lots more bonus content, all for free.

Get started by visiting: http://georgekayde.com/free-books/

Chapter One

"Listen up, pig," Alistair said, pointing at Ollie, who wiggled his pink snout in response. If Alistair didn't know any better, he'd think the animal was going through a rebellious phase like most adolescent boys and girls did. Better dealing with animals on a farm than with the haughty, snot-nosed knights visiting Teerdock all the way from Rowan. Even troublemaking animals like Ollie were preferred over one moment spent with the nobility.

"I'm only going to say this once." He pointed to the opened pen. "Get in there."

All the other animals were in their pens and cages in the barn. Most had gone off to eat their dinner. The rest stuck their wet snouts out, as if watching the spectacle between Alistair and Ollie unfold. Some animals chewed on hay and grass as humans would chew on nuts and grapes while watching a jousting tournament.

He slinked toward Ollie. Step by step, he closed the space between them. Ollie sniffed around the dirt, but Alistair knew the pig's eyes were on him, gauging the distance.

Now!

He rushed forward, swooping his arms down and around. But Ollie slipped through his grasp and Alistair crashed cheek first into the wood panel wall. Dust rained down from the pitched ceiling.

Alistair spun around, frustration lancing through him. "Everyone else has gone to their rightful place. The horses."

And, as if the horses knew they were called, they whinnied.

"The chickens."

Clucked.

"And the lambs."

Bleated.

Alistair took their sounds as agreement; they were on his side. "Even the other pigs."

Again, he went for Ollie. Round two. If only the men could see him now. Who'd ever believe a knight would lower himself to work as a common farmer? Or, for that matter, talk to pigs? It wasn't the stuff of legends, that was for sure. The Twelve Knights of Old didn't prattle with livestock.

"All your friends are there." He was so close now. Closer than before. This time Ollie was as good as his. "Don't you want to be with your friends?"

He lunged forward and this time caught Ollie in his arms. But he'd gone in too fast and his foot slipped on the dirt. He struggled to hold his balance while Ollie squealed in his ear. The pig kicked and bucked and wiggled out of Alistair's hold, just as Alistair tripped and fell on his ass.

Glaring, Alistair jumped back up. "Now you listen to me, pig." He brushed hay and grass from his trousers. "I am Alistair Rudell. They don't call me the Boar Knight for nothing."

He wasn't about to give up. What would Lorne think? The Boar Knight beaten by a troublesome piglet? Alistair would be the laughingstock of the Teerdock. "Animals bow down to me. I belong to a higher species than you. Understand? No, of course not. You're just a pig." He spat the last word out and Ollie oinked in reply. "A wily, inconsiderate, rebellious pig. You're the Black Knight of farm animals. But I'll get you…" He approached Ollie for a third—hopefully lucky—time. "Oh, yes. I'll get—"

He leapt. This time he'd engulf the pig, leaving nowhere for Ollie to run or hide. But Ollie was nothing if not slippery. Squealing, Ollie dashed away while Alistair was in mid-flight.

He hit the ground hard with a thump. A pungent, grotesque stench filled his nostrils. The fall wouldn't have been so bad, if Ollie hadn't been standing by the manure pile that Alistair had met with face first.

He spat and cursed. Silence reigned. Not a peep from the animals. He looked over at Ollie.

Something passed between them. Alistair couldn't tell if it was because of his murderous scowl, but Ollie apparently absorbed the severity of the situation. The fun and games were over, and Ollie sulked as he waddled to the pig pen, his snout lowered as if ashamed.

Alistair stood up and rubbed his face with the sleeve of his tunic. "There. See? Now was that so hard?" He closed the pen and locked it. Ollie looked up at him and made a noise, a kind of squeak. Alistair leaned over the wooden fence and petted the little pig's head.

With his work done, he went outside the barn where Lorne waited for him. "All animals accounted for."

"Including Ollie?" Lorne passed Alistair a wet cloth. It was as if he'd known Alistair would fall into the manure pile, like he'd had the same experience with Ollie before and prepared for it.

"Especially Ollie." Alistair cleaned his face. He'd have to wash himself thoroughly when he got back to his father's manor.

"I do appreciate it, Sir Alistair." Lorne stood hunched over, supporting his weight with a wooden cane.

"Just Alistair is fine. How's the back?"

"Stiff as a board." Lorne winced as he stretched from side to side, not moving very far in either direction. "'Fraid I can't bend over or pick up anything heavier than a cup of water."

"Take it easy, Lorne. You're not as young as you once were." Definitely not. Lorne looked as worn down as a leather jerkin. Decades of a farmer's life had taken its toll on him. "Maybe time to pass the farm to your son."

Lorne snorted. "That good-for-nothing? I just hope he spent most of the coin I gave him for the supplies we need from Bellamore and not on the mead he wants."

"Why go so far for mead?" Alistair asked, rhetorically. Bellamore was a town in the fiefdom north of Teerdock. Some Teerdock farmers sold their wares there and purchased what tools and supplies they couldn't find in Teerdock. "We have the best drinking establishments in all of the Rowanark Kingdom." Especially since the farmlands in Teerdock grew the best honey and grains for mead and beer. It was the primary export Teerdock had with the other fiefdoms, especially the more city-like ones that didn't have large farms.

Lorne patted Alistair on the back. "I appreciate all you've done."

They started walking toward Lorne's house, a timber framed building with wattle and mud walls.

"We all must pull our weight in Teerdock," Alistair said.

Lorne smiled at him. "You'd make a fine king someday."

That came at Alistair like a physical blow. "I'm just a knight." King? He'd take over as Duke of Teerdock from his father one day, but that was as far as his ambitions would lead him.

"Better a king. Maybe then we'd have a leader who wouldn't forget our poor village."

Alistair stopped and put his hands on Lorne's shoulders. "Not poor. Never poor. I prefer rustic. Sounds better." He winked and smiled. "I should be going."

The Rowanark nobles would arrive at Teerdock tonight. They had business with Alistair's father. He had to clean himself off and prepare himself for an unpleasant dinner. "Give Barbara my love."

"Sure you don't want to stay for dinner? It's the least I can do."

"Depends." Alistair glanced toward the barn. "Is it pork?"

"Porridge, I think. Barb's been at it all day. And she made extra, thinking my son would return today."

"Tempting, believe me. But I should be getting back." He started his way toward the manor.

"See you at Wendel's tonight?" Lorne asked.

"Does a bear shit in the woods?" Alistair grinned and waved goodbye. A night of drinking after putting up with the nobles would be just what he needed. "See you then. Enjoy your lovely wife's lovely cooking."

#

Alistair made it back to his father's manor. He strode through the main hall toward the bedrooms in the back, stopping by the pantry to pick up lemons and a cloth towel that he dampened with water. He found the hallways empty of either his father or Reynard, Alistair's knight-tutor and his father's retainer. They were probably preparing for the nobles' arrival. Reynard would don his best surcoat and look more noble than he usually did, which was pretty nose-in-the-air noble.

In his room, Alistair took off his shirt and switched his pants. He doused the wet cloth with lemon juice and started cleaning himself off from his scuffle with Ollie.

A knock sounded and the door opened. Reynard, and, as expected, he wore his fancy surcoat. The red brocade one. He always wore that one on special occasions.

"Playing with pigs again?" he said.

"Helping Lorne with his farm." Alistair dabbed his face, neck and bare chest with the lemon-scented cloth. As much as he liked the animals, he sure didn't want to smell like one.

"Lorne is a farmer and can work his own farm. You have duties here. Duties as a knight."

Alistair rolled his eyes. Wasn't the first time he'd heard that, and it wouldn't be the last time, either. As if his duties as a knight meant only placating privileged nobles. He was like them only in title, and nothing else. "Are they even here yet?"

"Not yet, but soon." Reynard always had the best posture. Squared off shoulders. Chin slightly pointed upward. Feet shoulder width apart. The man was a pillar, and he'd been hard on Alistair as his squire. He had graying hair, but was clean shaven, giving him a youthful appearance. "And I expect you on your best behavior."

"Oh, good. Just when I thought smelling like shit was going to be the worst part of my day, I have to have dinner with nobles."

"Make sure the stink is gone."

"I know. I know. I'll smell like lavender and peaches." Not quite. He'd smell vaguely of lemon and mostly like farm. He was probably the only knight who did smell like that, and he was fine with it.

"They're just knights," Reynard said. "Like you."

They're nothing like me. That had become clear to him during his time as a page in Rowan. He'd been raised differently from the other pages, and they made sure he knew it, making fun of him because of where he'd been born and who his father was, just a lord of a backwater fiefdom. Sure, he grew up in his father's manor, but calling it a manor was pushing it. His time as a squire, learning under Reynard, hadn't been that much better.

Reynard picked up Alistair's longsword from its place leaning against the wall in the farthest corner of the room, sentenced to collect dust. He inspected it, turning it from side to side. "When was the last time this was polished, let alone used?"

The sword had been a gift when Alistair had been knighted. He was supposed to have it with him to show his status in the kingdom as a knight, but he never had occasion to use it. It wasn't like he went on any quests outside of helping the farmers.

Alistair grabbed the longsword's blade and snatched it from Reynard. That would've been dangerous if the sword had been sharpened regularly, but truth was, it had been left alone for the past two years since his knighting. The thing was dull. Not any more dangerous than a child's wooden toy sword.

"Why are they coming here?" Alistair said, putting the sword back in its place. "Father usually goes to Rowan for meetings." He found himself a clean surcoat, a plain green one, and a pair of dark brown trousers. "Some council or whatever."

"King Hayden is sick."

"Sick?" With a cough? The sniffles? Or with something worse?

"We received news of this only recently."

Something worse, then. Why else have the nobles come here? They were likely traveling to all the fiefdoms, spreading news.

Alistair tied a leather belt around his waist. The news of King Hayden's failing health made him think of Princess Leera. He hadn't seen her since he'd graduated from page to squire. She loved her father more than anyone else in the world. Something in him ached to think about what she might be going through. He quelled those feelings, ignored them. He hadn't seen Leera in almost ten years, and she was, no doubt, like the rest of them. Snotty and pretentious.

A part of him hoped she wasn't, though.

"What's that to us?" he said. "We're all the way on the other side of Rowanark."

"Honestly," Reynard said, his voice grave, "I don't know."

"And honestly, I don't care. About the king or the rest of them." He adjusted the surcoat. It fit a lot tighter around his shoulders than he remembered. Hadn't worn the damnable thing in several months. "They don't care about us, why should we care about them?"

Reynard went up to him and helped him fit the surcoat comfortably, then dusted off the front with a few pats. "We are part of Rowanark Kingdom. Your father is a member of the Knight Council, just like you will be someday."

"I'd be happy to just stay here and never leave. I'll be sure to tell the knights where to stuff it."

Reynard's expression contorted and he grabbed Alistair by the collar and shook him. "Don't be such an arrogant brat! You're a knight. Act like one."

Reynard's eyes hardened, and his stare bore into Alistair. His fists were so tight around Alistair's surcoat, he could feel Reynard's knuckles on his neck. He didn't wear a scowl and his face remained calm, but his eyes smoldered. Alistair had never seen the look, not even when he'd been Reynard's squire, and, admittedly, he hadn't been the best, most easy to train boy.

Reynard let him go, shoving him back. "To think I tutored you to become a knight."

Alistair laughed. "Oh please, stop patting yourself on the back. The only reason you tutored me was because you had no choice. You've always hated Teerdock. Ever since you were sent here by King Hayden himself. A punishment, right?"

"Enough, Alistair."

"You're just like the nobles. You used to be one of them. A Rowan boy. Born and raised in the heart of the kingdom." Alistair bowed low. "Sorry we of lowly Teerdock can't be so accommodating for you, my prince."

"Act like a knight. For one dinner. I beg you."

Reynard's voice gave Alistair pause. It hadn't been a demand or an order, but a plea. Reynard hadn't chosen Alistair to be his squire or to live in Teerdock. No, he'd been sent there by the king. It had to have been some kind of banishment. Reynard had never told Alistair the full story.

In truth, Alistair had been thrilled he'd get to squire for the famous Sir Reynard, who had squired for King Hayden himself. There was not a better knight-tutor. But training under Reynard had turned out to be harsh, brutal even. The lessons hadn't been easy. Not the combat training in sword, bow and arrow, or the book learning in politics and history. Alistair had always figured Reynard resented his position in Teerdock and took it out on Alistair. He still respected Reynard, but he'd given up impressing his knight-tutor a long time ago. It didn't matter how good Alistair was with the sword or in war tactics, the words "I'm proud of you" never left Reynard's mouth.

A knock sounded at the door and Alistair's father poked his head into the room. "Here you two are."

"Father," Alistair said.

Reynard bowed. "My lord."

Alistair's father, Pydor, looked at Alistair from head to toe. Alistair had on his surcoat and a fresh pair of pants, but his feet were bare. "Why aren't you ready yet?"

"Your son doesn't want to go, my lord," Reynard said, hands clasped behind his back. He had returned to the militant, respectful, stick-in-the-butt Alistair was accustomed to. "He feels himself above those he claims treat others like footstools."

Pydor sighed and shook his head. Alistair's father was portly, with a jiggling chin. He'd never met a pastry he hadn't liked. "Not this again. You know, there was a time when you couldn't wait to be a page in Rowan."

"I was seven. I didn't know what I was getting myself into."

"And now you're twenty-three. A knight." Pydor shrugged. "Granted, not a practicing one."

"I help those in need." Wasn't that what a knight did?

Pydor looked down at the wet clothes on the stone floor, clearly spying the manure stains. "Yes. Very chivalrous of you, my son." Then he grabbed Alistair by his arms. "Listen to me, I know you hate this. I know you can't stand the nobles. But will you be cordial tonight with your fellow knights for me?"

Pydor had a desperate plea in his eyes and Alistair hated it; hated it because he was the cause of it. When did his father ever ask him for anything? Never. Not really, at least. And here he'd acted like a child. "How long are they staying?"

"Just the night. They'll be gone in the morning." He patted Alistair's shoulders. "Come on, they're not so bad. They don't bite, I swear."

Alistair sighed. "Fine. For you, I'll go." He couldn't deny his father. In truth, if his father told him the nobles were staying for a year and in his room, he would've done it. "But I'm not going to like it."

"Of course," Reynard said. "That would be asking for the impossible." He rolled his eyes and Alistair glared at him.

"Just make sure to smile and nod," Pydor said. "And try not to say much."

"Father! I'm not going to embarrass you."

"I know, I know. But not everyone is as used to your growl as Reynard and I are."

"Not to mention the pig," Reynard added.

#

Dinner was, ironically, pork.

The cooked beast sat in a bowl in the centre of the dining table within the great hall of the manor. Alistair sat with Reynard in the back, while his father took the head of the table. Eight nobles, all knights and dukes, lined the table on either side.

Alistair recognized some of them. Three had been fellow pages during his time at Rowan. Ivan from Bardon and Oswald from Grayden. And Destrian from Pendrakken. He couldn't quite remember Ivan or Oswald, but Destrian he would never forget. Who could forget the permanent smirk on Destrian's face or the way he looked at everyone like he was better than them? He'd been the quintessential noble. His father, who was also at the table, wasn't much better.

The nobles ate like the pig they feasted on. They chewed loudly, stuffed their faces with meat, and chucked any bones on the floor with disregard. They had no respect and it took everything in Alistair not to say something about it.

"I trust the food is to your liking?" Pydor asked.

"Not bad," Norwood said, wearing a smirk that matched his son's, "for Turd-dock."

The nobles chuckled, but Alistair wasn't impressed. "It's pronounced *Teer*dock," he said through gritted teeth. "Like the tears spilled after I punch you in the—"

Reynard kicked him under the table, shutting him up. They shared a glance and Alistair could read his eyes: *Behave yourself. Don't embarrass your father.*

For his father, he could suffer one dinner. Besides, his father could defend himself and didn't need his son to do it for him.

Norwood raised an eyebrow at Alistair. "Hm. I heard you became a knight, Alistair. What was your quest again? Herding cattle?"

More chuckles.

"I slew a wild boar that wrecked a few of our farms."

"Ah, that's why they call you the Boar Knight. Funny you were knighted for hunting animals. I suppose that's not your fault, though." Norwood directed his words to Reynard now. "That error lies with the knight you squired for."

Reynard remained perfectly stoic. He raised his chin. "I assure you, Sir Alistair earned his knighthood." His words were final, needing no further explanation.

"It was quite a large boar," Pydor said. "Fearsome beast. Nothing I'd ever seen before."

Norwood rolled his eyes and swirled his mead in his goblet. "And you grew up here, did you not, Pydor?"

"*Lord* Pydor," Alistair said.

Destrian smiled wolfishly at Alistair.

"My apologies," Norwood said. "Lord of Turd-dock."

Bastard. But before Alistair could say anything or correct him for a third time, Pydor piped in.

"I did grow up here. As my father did and his father before him. Been here for generations. It hasn't always been easy. But it's a simple life."

"I suppose it suits you." It wasn't a compliment.

Pydor cleared his throat. "So, what news from Rowan? How fares the king?"

Norwood dabbed his mouth with a kerchief. "The king is not well. He grows weaker by the day."

"That's terrible," Reynard said, his lips a thin line.

"Yes. Especially since his only heir is the Princess Leera. But I come bearing more news. King Hayden has declared that all fiefdoms and their knights shall participate in a jousting tournament."

Pydor's eyebrows lifted. "A jousting tournament?"

"We've never done that before," Reynard said. "To what end?"

"That's where things get interesting," Norwood said. "The tournament's champion will become the next heir to the throne."

The next King of Rowanark? This was no ordinary tournament.

"Can't Leera rule?" Alistair asked. Why have a king when you had a queen? Rowanark needed a ruler, yes, but either man or woman could rule. Leera would've had the same education in politics and warfare as any of the knights. She had been there at all the lessons with the other pages. She'd been a curious girl, and it was hard to imagine she'd somehow lost that inquisitive mind. She would've been by her father's side at all times, learning under him about how to rule the kingdom. That was real experience, more than any of the knights had.

"Alone? No. Rowanark needs a king. A strong king. The tournament will decide who among the knights of the Kingdom of Rowanark will be most suited. We all have noble blood. Any one of us could, by blood, be king. But King Hayden wants only the best, and so the competition will decide who will be Rowanark's next king when the current one has passed on."

"And what will happen with Princess Leera?" Alistair asked.

"She is to be wed to the tournament's winner."

A forced marriage. She could be married to Destrian if he won the tournament. That was cruel punishment. Leera was probably the only good thing left in Rowan, if her royal status hadn't butchered the girl he'd known as a page. She'd wanted so badly out of the castle's confinement. A girl of adventure, who'd wanted to travel and see beyond the Kingdom of Rowanark. She'd been a little rebellious in her youth, but who could blame her? Alistair would go mad if he was cooped up in the manor all day, every day.

"Are we to participate in this tournament?" Pydor asked.

"Of course." Norwood said. "It's why I'm here. Your son, the Boar Knight, may actually become the Boar King."

More mocking laughter.

Pydor looked at Alistair and hope glittered in his eyes. Hope for what? Did his father *want* him to be King of Rowanark? Pydor had never shown any indication of wanting the crown, neither for himself nor for his son. And Alistair cared little for kingship or for Rowanark. Teerdock was his home. Besides, what did he know about how to be a king? All he knew was what he'd learned in books and studying history. Alistair would sooner let Leera rule Rowanark than himself. He probably knew more than she did about war tactics and combat, but that wasn't the day-to-day requirement for a peaceful kingdom like Rowanark. Maybe she and Alistair could rule together?

Rule together? He was getting ahead of himself. First, he'd have to compete in the tournament, and he had no intention of competing.

"Not that any of us here thinks your son has a chance of winning. If he's anything like his father, he probably isn't much of a knight."

Alistair gave Norwood a dark look. All the things he wanted to say tingled at the tip of his tongue, but he forced himself to keep his mouth shut.

"My son," Pydor said, "is a far better knight than I ever was."

Finally, some back-bone in his father's tone.

"Really?" Norwood said, a hint of a smile on his face. "Tell me, boy. When was the last time you quested?"

The question should've been, when was the *first* time Alistair quested? Questing had been a tradition passed on by the Twelve Knights of Old, who, under the Goddess Cosima, had been tasked with protecting the people from, as legend would tell, the titans who had enslaved humankind. None of that happened now, and the titans were believed to have been vanquished by the Twelve Knights, banished to the Great Depths.

Alistair's last quest had been to slay the wild boar that made him a knight. He wasn't against helping people, only that his helping hand tended to stay within Teerdock. He followed the Knight's Code, even if it meant plowing a field rather than apprehending criminals.

Alistair kept quiet. He didn't want to risk saying something he shouldn't in a manner that was less than kind.

"So, I was right," Norwood said. "Just like your father." He sighed melodramatically. "If you'd only applied yourself more, Pydor, you might have been lord over one of the other…prosperous fiefdoms. Then maybe Lady Quinn would never have left you."

Alistair clenched his jaw. The Lady Quinn had been Alistair's mother. She had left Pydor when Alistair was a boy, before he'd become a page. She hadn't wanted this life.

His father made no reply. He bit his lip, his eyes downcast.

Say something, Father. Defend yourself! Prove them wrong.

But he just sat there quietly while the rest ate his food, drank his wine, and made a mess of his home.

Alistair squeezed his hands into fists. He opened his mouth—

Reynard gripped his fist, catching Alistair off guard. Reynard gave him a hard stare and shook his head ever so slightly.

Alistair looked at his father, the man he held in the highest regard. Higher than even the king himself. The father who'd raised him when his mother had left. The father who had always seen the positive in everything. The father who never pushed him and supported his every decision.

More laughter. More snickering. The disrespect to his father was unbearable. But Pydor was a better lord, a better man, than any of them.

Alistair had enough. These men weren't knights. Not a shred of nobility in them.

"Excuse me," he muttered, and stood up so fast his chair toppled behind him. Without a second glance, he stormed out of the great hall.

So much for good behavior.

At least he didn't punch anyone.

Chapter Two

Alistair sipped his mead and savoured the honey taste. He sat by the makeshift wood bar in Wendel's tavern. It wasn't really a tavern, just an old barn Wendel had converted for the villagers to come in and drink and be merry after a hard day out in the fields. Local farmers supplied Wendel with their meads and wines, making it a communal place.

Chatter and laughter filled the tavern, and Alistair lost himself in the noise. He sat alone but could've joined any of the tables. He knew everyone in Teerdock; knew their wives and children; knew their day-to-day struggles. For the most part, people were content in Teerdock. They worked from dawn till dusk, but Pydor was easy on their taxes. Everyone had to pay toward Rowanark, and Teerdock was no exception, but his father hadn't added an additional tax on them for the fiefdom alone.

Alistair downed the rest of his mead in a single gulp. He'd need a lot more than this one single cup to forget dinner with the nobles. He couldn't believe how they'd treated his father. They stepped all over him, and Pydor had let it happen. They'd laughed at him, to his *face*, at *his* dinner table. Not exactly *noble* behavior. No villager had ever acted that way. If Alistair were Duke of Teerdock, there was no way he'd stand for it. Nobles were supposed to act…well, nobly, weren't they?

His future lay here in Teerdock. Not with some ridiculous jousting tournament. Who would've thought a tournament would decide the next king? Had King Hayden gone mad? So what if he didn't have a son? Leera could rule. She was more than capable, especially if she still had that headstrong personality. She'd make a better ruler than any of the knights.

It was downright stupid. Imagining someone like Destrian winning sent a shiver down his spine. Destrian was too much like his father, Norwood: a prick.

"You want another?" Wendel asked him from behind the bar, pointing at Alistair's empty cup.

"Sure," Alistair said.

Wendel filled the cup with mead from the wooden keg behind the bar and passed it back to Alistair. Wendel looked every bit like the carpenter he was, rugged and muscular. "Heard Ollie made a mess of you."

"He definitely won this round." Alistair raised his cup in thanks.

Wendel sighed theatrically. "The great Boar Knight brought down by a piglet."

"He got lucky, that's all."

Someone banged a nearby table hard with the palm of his hand. His laughter was like a dog barking to herd sheep.

"Shouldn't you be with the other knights?" Wendel asked. Likely everyone knew about the Rowanark knights' visit. In a village as close-knit as Teerdock, secrets were few and news traveled fast. "You know? Questing and whatnot."

"And leave you guys? You need me."

Wendel leaned in and put a hand on Alistair's shoulder. "You forget, Alistair." His eyes were hard, but honest. "We've been living here since before this realm became Rowanark Kingdom, before your father became duke of this fiefdom."

Did that mean Alistair needed Teerdock more than Teerdock needed him?

Hah—tell that to Lorne and his bad back.

"What is a fiefdom, anyway?" Wendel said. "Used to be we were just a village. We fed off the land and helped each other. There were no knights, kings, or kingdoms. That was someone else's problem."

Alistair shrugged. "I was born here." He was one of them just as much as any other. He didn't have his own farm, but he worked on farms every day and spent more time with the villagers than he did in the manor. "I like it here. Is that so wrong?"

Wendel laughed. "Not at all. You're one of us, for sure. But you're also not." He pursed his lips. "It's hard to explain." Then he winked. "Blame my dumb villager brain."

"Huh," Alistair had just lifted his cup to his mouth when a girl bumped into him, dropping off a tray of used cups and plates on the bar top to be washed. Mead spilled from his mug onto his trousers.

"Pardon me, your knightship," said the girl, Ava. She had long, dark hair and eyes as green as the pasture. She was one of the serving girls Wendel had hired, and had a reputation as a flirt. She made heads turn whenever she passed a table.

Before she bounded off, Wendel called after her. "Hey now, lady fair. What's the rush for? Stay. My friend here needs company."

She leaned into Alistair, giving him a seductive look. "Does he now?"

Ava was a pretty girl, no doubt. But when he looked at her, he couldn't help but compare her to Leera. Once upon a time, when he'd been a naïve page, he had promised himself that he'd marry Leera. He smirked. What a childish thing to believe, even if she had been the first girl to make his heart skip a beat.

"You know, he's a knight," Wendel said, with a curved smile on his lips. "Gonna be lord someday."

Playing his part, Alistair sat straighter on the stool, his shoulders squared off.

"You don't say? Lord of Teerdock?" Ava blew air between her cheeks. "Like that would get me very far. Who would want to be with the lord of this dump?"

Alistair gave her a flat look. So Wendel thought he didn't quite have a place in Teerdock and Ava thought he wasn't quite a noble. Where did he fit then? Was he going to be a forgotten lord of a forgotten village where even the villagers wouldn't need him? That wasn't much of a life.

Maybe Reynard was right. Maybe he should take his duties as a knight more seriously.

She brushed her long hair over her shoulder. Her eye caught someone and her face took on a different expression. Dreamlike. "He, on the other hand, is more to my liking."

All went quiet and Alistair turned around, fearing the worst.

Destrian, flanked by Ivan and Oswald, had come in and dashed away the farmers' merriment. The raucous laughter and endless chatter vanished.

"If you'll excuse me, boys," Ava said, clearly taken by Destrian and company and the splendour of their surcoats and full-length, fur-trimmed cloaks. Their swords, the hilts bedecked with shining jewels, were leather-bound and hung from their belts.

Wendel leaned forward toward Alistair. "Friends of yours?"

"No friends of mine, I assure you."

What are they doing here? Alistair lowered his chin and hunched over his drink.

Ava sat the nobles at one of the round tables. The chatter started up again, but more subdued than before. Wendel poured mead into fresh cups for them. Maybe they'd simply come for a friendly drink. Teerdock was known for its mead, after all. So long as they didn't bother him and he didn't bother them, everything would be just fine.

"I wondered where the knight of Teerdock had run off to."

Or maybe not.

Alistair groaned. He turned on his stool. Destrian stood with his goons on either side of him. He had a smug look on his face. He always had that look, coupled with an air of superiority. He would've benefited from a spanking or two when he was a child, but he came off as someone who always got his way. He was a dandy. He'd even let the nail of his pinky finger grow longer than the rest, a sign that his hands never touched a day's worth of hard labor.

Alistair hadn't liked him when they'd been pages, and he sure as all the Great Depths didn't like him now.

"Well, you found me." He kept his tone calm, though inside was anything but.

"Yes, in this filth." Destrian sipped his mead then spat it out. "Tastes like cow's piss!"

His goons laughed and Destrian snarled like a wolf. Even if he thought the mead had tasted delicious he would've said the same thing. He was trying to get a reaction from Alistair.

He wouldn't.

He got a rise out of the other villagers, though. The bigger, muscular villagers started to stand, glares clear on their faces.

The last thing Alistair wanted was for the villagers to get into a fight with nobility. This was about him and Destrian. They'd never gotten along. Alistair had grown up in Teerdock, but Destrian had grown up in a wealthy fiefdom. Pendrakken was next only to Rowan itself.

"Spoken from experience, I take it?" Alistair said.

Destrian narrowed his eyes at him. His lip twitched. "You're all words, Alistair. All talk. You always were." The tavern fell quiet again, all eyes and ears on Destrian. "Even when we were pages, you thought you'd become some great knight. But look at you now. Sitting in a barn, drinking cow's piss."

Alistair turned away from him. He'd promised his father he'd behave, and that meant shutting his mouth and keeping to himself.

"We always knew you'd amount to nothing." Destrian leaned into him and sniffed. "You still stink."

Those words flashed a memory in Alistair's mind: a group of pages led by Destrian bullying Alistair, making him feel worthless, making him feel like he didn't belong.

"You stink like a farm animal. You're nothing but cattle. You think *you're* a knight?" A snicker. "Please. Reynard only made you a knight because he felt sorry for you. Who becomes a knight by herding animals?"

Wendel's face reddened with anger. He opened his mouth to say something, but Alistair shook his head no and stopped him.

Just let him talk.

"Even if you did participate in the tournament, there's no way you'd succeed. You're weak. All you'll ever amount to is a lifetime of farming, like a good-for-nothing peasant."

The whole tavern brimmed with hatred. It was damn near palpable. They wanted to say something, do something, but what could a commoner do to a knight? It was a criminal offense to assault a knight, a member of the nobility.

Alistair's grip on his cup tightened, to the point where his fingers might break through the clay.

Again Destrian leaned in and whispered in Alistair's ear. "No one wants you. No one needs you. You're just like your useless father."

Alistair's fist tightened. Make fun of him, fine, but he wasn't going to let Destrian soil his father's reputation.

He threw a punch, but Destrian leapt back and Alistair hit air. Destrian smiled mirthlessly.

Alistair charged after him.

Destrian danced out of the way and kicked his leg out. Before Alistair could stop himself, he tripped over Destrian's foot. He shot his hands out and broke his fall. His palms burned as they skidded on the rough ground.

He spun around and started to get up but Destrian slammed his boot down on him, keeping him pinned on his back. Destrian leaned over, his weight crushing Alistair.

Alistair tensed, struggling to suck air into his lungs.

"You'll never be a real knight, let alone a king," Destrian said, then spat at him. "Just sit here and wait out your days as a farm boy, never amounting to anything. When I win the tournament and become crowned king, I look forward to having you as my loyal subject." He leaned down, his weight crushing Alistair painfully. "Get used to being beneath me. It's where you belong."

Ivan and Oswald barked a laugh. Destrian lifted his boot off Alistair's chest and Alistair gasped for air.

Two farmers helped him up. He glared at Destrian's retreating back.

Not a real knight? Just a good-for-nothing peasant?

Wait and see.

#

Alistair pounded on the door to his father's bedchamber. The room next to Pydor's opened and Reynard poked his head out of his own room.

"What's gotten into you?" Reynard asked.

"I'm going to do it!" Alistair said. Damn Destrian. Alistair would rather live in a pig pen with Ollie than let Destrian take the crown. His fist rapped on the door repeatedly.

"Do what?"

The door swung open and Pydor tied his robe around his waist, his nightcap sitting snugly on his balding head. He blinked, darting looks to either side of the hallway before settling on Alistair.

Alistair burst into the room. "I'm going to do it!"

"Do what?" Pydor asked.

Reynard came into the room, his face drawn, and tired.

Pydor closed the door behind them.

Alistair paced back and forth. "I'm going to go to Rowan and compete in the tournament."

Pydor sighed. "That's very brave of you, my son. But you don't have to go. I know how much you hate Rowan and the nobles."

"These are well trained knights you'd be going up against," Reynard crossed his arms over his chest. "As your knight-tutor, it pains me to admit this, but I don't think you're ready."

"I can beat them," Alistair said. Destrian had gotten the best of him tonight, but so what? Destrian had won a bar fight, but not the tournament. "Didn't I take to your lessons easily?"

Reynard nodded. Alistair was trained in combat skills. The sword. The lance. The bow and arrow. The axe. Even his bare hands. "But when was the last time you put on a suit of armor?"

Alistair rubbed his chin. "I don't have a suit of armor."

Reynard rolled his eyes. "Exactly my point."

"You would have to stay in Rowan," Pydor said, "in the castle, with the other knights. And if you won, you would be King of Rowanark and would have to stay there and rule."

King? Oh, no, he had no intention of taking the crown. All he wanted was to prove to the nobles that he was their better. That he had as much of a right to call himself a knight and a noble as they did. Then Leera could take the crown for herself. The crown rightfully belonged to her, and she could marry whomever she wished.

"You said it yourself, Father, there was a time I looked forward to going to Rowan."

"But you haven't been back since you were a page. You didn't even go back when you were knighted, like you were supposed to."

"I've changed," Alistair said.

Pydor tilted his head. "People don't change overnight."

"You're right." But this hadn't been overnight. It had been building since he was seven years old. He'd believed in a nobility that no longer existed. The knight he'd wanted to become no longer quested in the Kingdom of Rowanark. The Knight's Code, that ancient code that had been bestowed upon all knights from Cosima, the Mother of Knighthood, was no more than a farce, and none of those snot-nosed nobles could live up to it. That was the reason he'd ignored his duties as a knight, because he didn't want to be associated with the likes of Destrian. He took his father's hand in his. "But I saw that look you gave me at dinner. You want me to go."

And perhaps, more than anything, he wanted to make his father proud.

"Alistair…"

"I didn't quite understand why you wanted me to go. But I get it now. You want me to have a shot at a better life. You want more for me than Teerdock. I love it here, Father, it's true, but maybe there is more for me. I've become restless of late and swiftly irritated at every little thing."

"I can attest to that," Reynard remarked.

Alistair shot Reynard a withering look before turning back to Pydor. "Let me do this. Let me prove to you that I can be the knight you want me to be. Let me make you proud. Let me show Pendrakken and Rowan and all the other fiefdoms what a real knight can do."

A smile spread across Pydor's cheeks, but behind that smile was a note of sadness. "I could never give you the life I wanted to give you. The life your mother wanted."

"It's not your fault." Pydor had tried to give both him and his mother everything he could with the power he'd been given. It had been a good life. "You did the best you could. I'd say you even spoiled me." He glanced over at Reynard to see if he'd make a smart remark, but he didn't. "So can I go?"

"Of course, you can go. You can take my armor and my horse, too."

Alistair surveyed his father from head to toe. "I hope it fits."

Pydor winked, rubbing his round belly. "I was once as skinny as you are now."

His father pulled him in for an embrace and squeezed him tightly, the way he used to when Alistair was a child. It used to embarrass him, but now he wrapped his arms around his father and squeezed back just as tightly.

Reynard put a hand on Alistair's shoulder. "I have to say, I'm impressed. I didn't think you'd come around."

"I'm sure you'll be glad to have me out of the manor," Alistair said.

Reynard chuckled. "Good luck in Rowan. This place won't be the same without you and the subtle smell of pig's shit."

Pydor narrowed his eyes and rubbed his chin. "Don't be so quick to say goodbye, Reynard."

Reynard blinked. "My lord?"

"You're going with him." Pydor patted Reynard's shoulder. "He'll need a herald."

"A herald, my lord?"

"Every knight in a tournament needs a herald," Pydor said, "and who better than his knight-tutor?"

"You're joking," Reynard said, then paused. "You're not joking."

Alistair nudged Reynard. "Guess you can help me put my armor on."

Reynard groaned. "Lovely."

Chapter Three

What was the point of being a princess, the daughter of the most powerful man in the kingdom, when you didn't have any power yourself?

Leera had spent her entire life debating that question, never finding an answer. She blew air between her cheeks.

"Don't sigh like that, darling," her mother, Queen Ursula, said. "It's unbecoming for a princess."

"Sorry, Mother." Leera sighed once more, this time with theatrical grace. "Better?"

Ursula lifted an eyebrow at her, clearly unimpressed.

Harsh, terrible coughing gripped both their attentions. It came from her father, King Hayden, who lay in the canopy bed within his chamber.

Ursula, a frown settling deep around her mouth and brow, sat on the feathered mattress and wiped his mouth with a cloth. Leera sat in a chair on the opposite side of the bed. Seeing her father cough like that, like he'd break a rib, and his clammy skin and the dark circles under his eyes left Leera feeling more worthless than ever before.

A princess with no power. She was a title and nothing more. She'd trade it all in to have her father's health back.

"How are you feeling today?" she asked him.

"I could do without the sighing," King Hayden said. At least his tone was still strong. He had a voice akin to a lion's roar. Not necessarily loud, but commanding.

"I'm practicing swooning over the knights," Leera said.

"I don't know where you learned to lie so well." Hayden winked at Ursula. "Must've been your side of the family."

Her father meant it as a joke, yet Leera could see the stab of hurt—no, guilt—on her mother's face. Even when her mother frowned, she was still beautiful. Leera had her mother's svelte figure and long thick hair, but she took most of her facial features from her father—icy blue eyes, high cheek bones, and a delicate nose.

"I learned from my father," Leera said as she got up from her chair to sit on the bed next to Hayden. "I've seen you during petitions. Pretending to care."

"I do care. For the first fifteen. Then it sort of drags on. It's not easy being king."

Wasn't that the truth. Since her father's illness had gotten worse, Leera had been taking over her father's duties. The king's chancellors didn't much like it and would whisper advice in her ear after hearing a petition. But she'd spent most days with Hayden, learning from him by watching and absorbing what he did and how he spoke to his people. It came naturally to her. Much more naturally than reviewing the scrolls with the kingdom's taxes. There she needed the help of those more suited to mathematics. Regardless, she understood where the taxes ought to go to benefit the kingdom at large.

Resolving civil disputes, taxes, ensuring the kingdom flourished—those were all things she'd gained a fast understanding in. It wasn't quite like the books she'd studied, but the education she'd had gave her the critical mind she needed to make sound judgements. What she hadn't dealt with, and what she hoped she'd never have to do deal with, was war. The Kingdom of Rowanark had been peaceful since her birth and she'd like to keep it that way. "Maybe I ought to marry someone with endless amounts of patience," Leera said.

"And heart. Not like your heartless father." Hayden reached into the sleeve of his robe and pulled out a single stemmed lily, as gold as her hair was, and offered it to Leera. She took it with a giggle, the kind of giggle she'd made when she first saw that magic trick years ago, when she was a little girl. He was always playing tricks on her. She didn't know where he'd learned them or how he did them. When asked, he'd give her a wink and say, "A wizard never tells his secrets."

Apparently, neither did wizard kings like her father.

"Better to have boring petitions during times of peace than endless declarations during a war," Ursula said.

"Truth in that." Hayden looked out at the sunlight streaming in through the chamber window. Outside, birdsong filled the skies. A faraway gleam filled Hayden's eyes. No doubt her father thought back to the times when there wasn't peace, before she was even born. When her father warred against the Black Knight, conquering him by uniting the fiefdoms into one single kingdom and he that kingdom's king.

He started coughing again, his face contorting, his body convulsing with each hack of breath. They said her father was a hero. All the ballads and songs said so. The greatest knight in all the kingdom.

There was no one who could replace him.

"I think you should stay in bed," Ursula said, dabbing Hayden's brow with a wet cloth. "Let one of the Dukes make the welcoming speech."

The knights from the fiefdoms arrived today for the tournament. They'd all be gathered in the castle's inner ward.

"I could always do it," Leera said.

"Nonsense. I invited everyone. I must address them. I'm fine. Truly." As if to prove his point, Hayden propped himself up on his bed. "I just got a little winded, that's all."

"It's a stupid contest, anyway," Ursula said.

"I agree," Leera said. "I should marry whomever I want."

"Leera should marry Destrian."

Leera gave her mother a jaw-dropping look. "*What?*"

"He's the perfect knight. Learned, strong. Comes from a fiefdom that is as big as Rowan itself. I can't think of a more suitable candidate."

"*Candidate.*" The word tasted bitter. "That's what we're calling my future husband?"

"He does come to the Knight Council with his father," Hayden said, joining sides with Ursula. "Can't say that about all the knights."

"Of course, he comes. Pendrakken is right next door to us. The ride is less than a day to and from. I could walk there for Cosima's sake!"

"Leera!" Ursula said. "Watch your tongue."

"I can't watch my tongue, Mother. If I could, you'd probably tell me to stop watching my tongue." She demonstrated by sticking her tongue out and looking down at it, which probably made her eyes cross.

Hayden chuckled. "He's tall, dark and handsome."

"He's looming, menacing, and…okay, he's handsome."

She didn't have a problem with Destrian, but every time he came to the castle, he had some gift for her. Jewelry or flowers, but usually jewelry. It was always too much. It drove her crazy. As if a gold bracelet would make her fall in love with him. She had a drawer filled to the brim with gold trinkets, most of them—she hated to admit—from Destrian.

Good looking, fine, but not particularly charming.

Hayden chuckled again, but it quickly descended into a coughing fit so harsh he spat out blood.

Ursula jumped to her feet, worry lines creasing her face. "I'll get the doctor."

As her mother fled the chamber, Leera came up to Hayden and wiped the blood from his chin and neck. Not yet noon and already her father looked weary. "You know what I hate most about this tournament, Father?"

"What's that, my love?"

"What it means for you."

Hayden rubbed her cheek with a bony knuckle and smiled at her, a smile that had more sadness in it than it ought.

Leera smiled to staunch tears.

Ursula came back with the doctor in tow. Leera kissed her father's forehead and left the chamber.

She wandered the castle hallways, restless as ever. The castle was as much her home as it was her prison. She was stuck, not allowed to leave the castle on her own without an escort, which usually meant a handful of guards. Not exactly what she'd call fun.

She went to the kitchens and ate some fruit, then to the stables and petted her horse, Snapper, then to the library, where she tried to find a book or a scroll she hadn't at least glanced at before. She came up with nothing.

Next, she went to the chapel within the rear west wing of the castle. She sat down by the pews and closed her eyes. Soon she would know who her husband would be, what her future would entail. The thought sent her heart into a gallop. If only she could become a priestess and devote her life to the Way of Cosima, then she wouldn't have to get married. She could leave the castle and travel the kingdom, singing the stories and words of the Lady Cosima and her Twelve Knights of Old.

Funny how a priestess had more freedom than a princess.

She opened her eyes and stared up at the twelve-pointed star representing Cosima's knights. Maybe she ought to pray. She clasped her hands together. *Dear Cosima, please cancel the tournament. Dear*

Cosima, please give me the strength to make my own decisions.

Dear Cosima, please cure my father. Please.

"It's good to see you here, Princess."

Leera yelped. "Stellios. You scared me." She took a moment to catch her breath. Stellios was the chief priest in Rowanark Castle. "You might see me here more often."

"Oh?"

"I'm thinking of joining the priesthood."

Stellios chuckled. "Not too happy about the tournament?"

"Not particularly."

"I understand." He grimaced. "It's barbaric."

Leera nodded. "Thank you."

"You should just marry Destrian."

"Stellios!"

"He's a good knight. Donates to the chapel quite frequently. In fact, that star was made using the money he gave."

Leera rolled her eyes. "He's a saint."

"I wouldn't go that far. But he's a catch, all right."

Then you marry him, was what she wanted to say, but stayed silent instead.

Stellios left her to pray. A trio of priestesses came into the chapel and Leera watched them with an eagle's eye. They walked in, bowed in front of the Twelfth Star, and fled into an antechamber. Before the door closed behind them, Leera caught the sight of a priestess's habit hanging near the door and it sparked an idea.

She waited another ten minutes. When quiet descended, she tiptoed to the antechamber and, first checking behind her to see that no one watched, opened the door. The habit hung an arm's reach from her. She grabbed it, folded it up, and went to her room.

The habit clung tightly around her waist. Every step she took, Leera risked ripping the material. If Leera did become queen, the first thing she'd do would be to abolish all fasting, whether for religion or otherwise. Honestly, this habit was made for a quill, not a person.

She started her way toward the barbican. Clinging and clanging sounds rang in the hall. Plated armor and chain mail, she was sure of it. Knights.

She lowered her head, and kept going. A veil covered most of her face except for her eyes. The noise grew louder and louder, then stopped when she bumped headfirst into a hard surface.

Great. She'd managed to run right into the very people she wanted to avoid.

Knights.

"My apologies," she said, her ears burning. She kept her head low.

"You ought to watch where you're going, sister," said the knight.

She recognized the voice. It was musical, but more like a dirge than a sweet melody. Destrian. Now she definitely didn't look up.

She lowered her head even more. Of all the knights—why Destrian?

"I'll remember that," she said, changing her tone so she sounded like a mouse. She grimaced. It sounded fake to her ears.

Destrian put a gloved finger below her chin and lifted her head. She had no choice but to met his steely gaze with her own. Thank Cosima, she wore the veil. Hopefully, it'd be enough to conceal her identity.

Destrian looked at her for what seemed like several long, dragging minutes. He really was handsome, dashing, even pretty, but he was cold. She'd never seen him smile. No, that wasn't true. He'd smiled plenty of times, but never with joy. Just like his father, Norwood. Incapable of joy, but capable of pretending it.

"You have pretty eyes," he said to her.

She resisted the urge to roll those pretty eyes of hers. "Thank you, my lord."

He lowered his hand, his eyes drinking her in. "A shame you chose this life. You could've made a fine wife to a very happy man."

"I am devoted to the Way of Cosima," Leera said, bowing her head once more and making the sign of the Twelfth Star.

"Praiseworthy. You may leave."

"Thank you." She scurried around him and was almost through the gates and into freedom.

"Wait a moment. Hold on."

She halted and squeezed her eyes shut. He must've seen through her disguise after all. She turned around, slowly. "Yes, my lord?"

"I thought priestesses weren't supposed to leave the chapel?" Destrian asked.

"You have priestesses confused with princesses," said Leera. "A princess can't leave a castle." *And don't I know it.* "A priestess can go wherever she likes." *Pretty much.* "Spread the good word, as it were."

Destrian considered that a moment, then nodded. "Right. Well, good luck."

She bowed, turned on her heel, and passed through the castle gates.

#

Compared to the cold, dreary, and predictable castle, the city was anything but. The sun's rays blazed down on the cobblestone streets and Leera never ran into the same people twice. There was always something different in the city, something she hadn't seen before. People or buildings, shops and trinkets. She had no idea how many people resided in the city, but she figured the number had to be in the thousands, maybe tens of thousands.

She couldn't walk the city streets unless guards escorted her, and that was more limiting than freeing. She was the only heir that King Hayden had sired, so she had to be protected at all costs. As if there were any real dangers here now that the Black Knight had been vanquished by her father. And it wasn't like she'd get to rule as queen, anyway. The winner of the tournament, some duke's son, would take over Rowanark.

It had better not be Destrian. Pretty eyes? To a priestess? To say that was inappropriate would be an understatement. It nearly made her cringe.

She usually visited the city with an escort, but often she went to the city disguised as someone other than the princess. Today marked the first day she'd traveled as a priestess and she rather liked the people's bowed heads as they passed by her. It meant no one paid a close eye to her and just let her be. She normally dressed up in plain clothes, a homespun dress she'd take from one of the castle maids, and tried to look like any ordinary person walking the streets. She'd even dressed as a beggar once. But her riskiest disguise had been donning the tabard and helmet of a castle guard. The helmet had been a bit big on her, though, and the ordeal had left her with an achy neck for a few days. It was nice pretending to be someone other than the princess, and she got a kick out of playing tricks and seeing how far she could go with it. She figured she got that trait from her father, but where her father was into magic tricks, she was into disguises. The two of them ought to start their own traveling troupe.

She loved the market quarter the most. It was noisy and smelly and a bit on the dirty side, but there were people from all over the kingdom. She liked to hear the merchants call out their wares and what fiefdom those wares came from. She'd never had a chance to visit any of the other fiefdoms, but she got to know them through what was sold here. Like the soft, silky dresses and outlandish pointy hats that told her the people of Neblium must be fashionable. Or the olive oils from the warmer fiefdom of Aithin, which put the image in her head of hills full of olive trees.

She stopped at a fresh fruit stand selling apples, pears and fresh berries. She picked up a pear and gave it a squeeze. Firm and bright green colored.

"Take it, sister," the merchant said, a man with bushy eyebrows and long nose. "It's yours. For free."

"Thank you," Leera said. Being a priestess had its perks. She bit into the pear and let the juices fill her mouth. Delicious.

She raised an eyebroabw and scanned the other stalls. What else could she get for free? She eyed the jewelry next. Servants of Cosima needed a little gold glow to them, didn't they?

Then she heard the voice of a man she could've sworn she knew. His voice froze her solid.

"This damn armor keeps piercing my back!"

The voice sounded a bit deeper than she remembered. More mature sounding, even if his words were anything but.

"So much for fitting into your father's armor," a new voice said, this one unfamiliar.

"Must I wear this now?"

"We're about to go to the tournament ceremony, so yes, you must wear it now."

Leera turned around and couldn't believe her eyes. Alistair Rudell, the knight who was supposed to steal her away from the castle back when he was just a page and she a young, restless princess. She hadn't seen him since that time. He stood awkwardly, his back arched and his face contorted. It was plain to see that the armor he wore was too small for his shoulders and chest.

"I swear this breastplate is an iron maiden," he said.

"If you complain about the armor one more time…" said the other man, older than Alistair with long, graying hair. He was tall and thin and stood like a knight, proud and unwavering. Though she'd never met the man, she guessed he was Reynard Trevault from what she knew of Teerdock.

"What? What are you going to do? You're *my* herald. You're supposed to listen to *me*."

Reynard cocked an eyebrow. "Do you even know what a herald is?"

Alistair's eyes rolled skyward as if the answer he looked for was in the sky. "It's like a squire."

"Nothing like a squire. Come on, we're going to be late."

Reynard started down the street toward the castle.

Alistair followed him but then stopped. His gaze met Leera's and he narrowed his eyes at her, as if he recognized her, too, but couldn't quite place her. But that was impossible. Through her disguise, all he could see was her eyes. The veil covered the rest. Besides, they hadn't seen each other in almost a decade.

But he didn't move and didn't break contact. She didn't either, and found herself admiring, of all things, his chin. It was square shaped and led to a strong, sculpted jaw line. Completely and utterly masculine. It framed the rest of his stubbly, rugged, and yes, oh so strikingly handsome face.

They must have been staring at each other for a full minute. That was okay with her. She could stare at him all day.

Wait—what was she thinking?

Then, farther down the road, past Alistair, castle guards marched toward them, asking merchants if they had seen a priestess pass through recently.

As much as she enjoyed the staring contest with Alistair, she had to leave. Her time in the city may have drawn itself to a close, but she didn't want to get caught and sent back with the guards. If she did get herself caught, her mother might assign her an escort at all times. She'd never been caught before and today would be no different.

So, she did the only thing a self-respecting princess could do, she turned around and started running—

And smacked right into a horse.

She fell over and the huge black charger whinnied and rose on its hind legs. Horseshoes kicked out at her.

I'm going to be trampled!

She squeezed her eyes shut, but the giant mass didn't come crashing down on her. Someone grabbed her and the two of them rolled across the cobblestones seconds before the horse landed.

She stopped rolling, lying on her back. Alistair hovered over her, using his hands to prop himself up.

They were still close. Close enough to admire his forest green eyes that went with his light blond hair. His honey-scented breath caressed her cheeks, her nose, her mouth.

It felt…good.

They stayed like that for an overly long time. A small crowd gathered around them.

Taking notice, Alistair pushed himself up. "Since when did the Princess of Rowanark become a priestess?" Alistair said, offering his hand to her.

A cool breeze blew across Leera's face. Her veil. It was missing. It must've flown off her face.

Alistair wore a self-amused grin. He was proud of himself. A little too proud. Like he'd found a treasure that no one else could find.

She glared at him and slapped his hand away, getting up on her own. "It's been a long time." She brushed the dirt from her dress. "I'm married to the Way of Cosima now."

"Really? Do the knights of the tournament know?"

"You've got some nerve." Leera started walking.

Alistair followed her step for step. "For rescuing you?" He slapped his forehead. "What was I thinking? Should've let you get trampled by that horse."

"You're villainous."

"And you're beautiful."

She stopped short and spun toward him. Was he…flirting with her? Judging by the wry curve of his lips, the answer to that question was a resounding yes.

The guards drew closer. She had no time to stand there and dilly dally. She had to get back to the castle unseen. Alistair followed her gaze and saw the guards as well.

"I see you finally got out of that dusty old castle," he said.

"Didn't need your help after all," she said and resumed walking. The first time she'd tried to escape the castle was back when she was twelve years old and Alistair was fourteen, about to graduate from page to squire. He'd agreed to help her escape the castle, and would have if they both hadn't been caught. Alistair had gotten the brunt of the punishment, mostly from his fellow pages, who'd treated him like he didn't deserve to be called a page or squire or be part of the nobility. They'd been cruel to him, calling him names and saying he smelled like dirty farm animals. But he didn't, and he never had. He always smelled like honey, and there was no better smell than that.

"Maybe not," Alistair said, keeping pace, "but an escort wouldn't hurt."

"I like to be alone," she lied.

Alistair smirked. "No, you don't. If you did, you'd still be holed up in the castle."

"Don't pretend like you know me. It's been—"

"Nearly ten years. Do I look different?"

She gave him a glance from head to toe. He did look different. Mature and a lot bigger than he used to be. He had bronze skin from being out in the sun. But the armor he wore didn't suit him at all.

"You look uncomfortable."

Alistair laughed and tugged at his breastplate. "Believe me, I am. It's good to see you again. I should've come here sooner."

"Why didn't you?"

"I thought I had nothing left in Rowanark. Seems I was wrong."

Heat flushed her cheeks. "You don't have me, Alistair." Even if back in the day he'd said he would one day be a great knight and then king, which meant he'd be married to her. That was then, though, and they'd just been children.

"Right, the tournament." He rolled his eyes. "I forgot."

"Princess!"

She stopped and grimaced. For two reasons, one, they had found her and her day of fun as a priestess was over, and two, Destrian was with the guards. "Oh, damn it."

Alistair nudged her with his elbow. "Hey, priestesses aren't supposed to swear."

"This is worth an exception."

They turned around to face the rustling chain mail and pounding boots. Six guards and Destrian greeted them. Alistair's expression clouded over, and he gave Destrian a dark look. Did the two know each other?

Of course, they did. Destrian had been at the forefront of Alistair's childhood torment.

"Princess, are you all right?" Destrian presumed to put his hands on her arms. Concern colored his voice, but was it real or pretended? "You were missing from the castle. Your father sent me and some of the guards to come looking for you."

"I'm fine," Leera said. "I had Sir Alistair here with me."

Destrian gave him a disgusted look. "Decided to partake in the tournament after all?"

"And miss an opportunity to finish what we started? Not likely."

What was started? Disappointed cut through her. And to think Alistair had led her to believe he'd come here for her, not some revenge attempt against Destrian.

Besides, why should she be disappointed? He was nothing to her but a childhood memory.

"Come, Princess," Destrian said, taking her by the arm, his grip like a manacle. "I am to escort you back to the castle."

"I know the way back to my own castle," Leera said with more spite in her tone than she had intended.

"It's not safe for the princess to be outside."

"Why?" Alistair asked. "These are her people. Is this enemy territory?"

Exactly. She was going to be these people's queen. She shouldn't fear them.

"Not all people respect the crown," Destrian said. "You should understand that."

Alistair winked at Leera. "I guess I'm anti-crown. Look at me, I can't even fit in my own armor. Sad excuse for a knight."

"Maybe you'd make a better king," Leera said.

Alistair threw his hands up, shrugging casually. "So they tell me."

Destrian had to practically drag her away.

Leera glanced back at Alistair, who stood there watching her until the crowds closed in and they couldn't see each other anymore.

Chapter Four

Alistair and Reynard arrived in the castle ward. Knights and their squires and heralds and even some of the fiefdom dukes were there. Chatter engulfed the ward, and old friends who hadn't seen each other in a long time, probably since graduating to squires, were catching up.

Alistair stood at the periphery, his arms folded over his breastplate, calling as little attention to himself as possible. The last thing he needed, or wanted, was a repeat of his time as a page. Even if they were all adults now—knights even—he didn't underestimate their capacity for childish bullying. And decked out in his father's choking, crushing, damnably uncomfortable armor, the knights would easily find something to poke fun about. At least his horse, a beautiful charger named Hale, had a shiny coat and toned muscles. His father took exceptional care of Hale.

He saw old enemies and old friends, albeit, mostly old enemies. They noticed him, cast one glance at his tabard embroidered with the Teerdock coat of arms—the sign of a boar—and gave him a look one might give to fungus.

"Glad to see not much has changed," Alistair said sarcastically.

Reynard gestured dismissively. "Ignore them." He received the same disgusted looks. They weren't off to a popular start. To his credit, Reynard stood with his chin held high. "Beat them on the lists."

Alistair nodded. Speaking of the lists, Rowanark pages and squires were already setting up the wooden barriers. The ward was huge, almost as large as a farming field. Alistair had first learned to use the sword in the ward back when he was a page. The sword's heaviness had shocked him. He'd managed a swing or two before it exhausted him.

Ah, those were the good old days.

Not truly.

"I can't believe it's you." The voice came from beside him.

Alistair turned to look. "Kythe?"

"It's me."

Alistair laughed and grabbed his old friend in an embrace. Out of all the pages Alistair had grown up with, Kythe had been the most kind. Everyone had liked him. He was funny, charming, and the youngest of all the pages, so everyone treated him like a younger brother. He still looked impossibly young. Clean shaven. Baby cheeks. Short and skinny, too.

"It's good to see a friendly face," Alistair said.

"No one thought you'd come."

"*I* didn't think I'd come."

"There was even a bet."

"I've always been the centre of attention around here."

"Not always good attention." Kythe patted him on the plated shoulder. "You look good. Except for that armor."

"It's my father's." Which was not the best excuse.

Kythe furrowed his brow. "Don't have a set of your own?"

"Not really, no. I prefer a good cotton tunic to all this heavy plated stuff."

"Guess it's true what they say," Kythe said with a whisper of a smile. "You slew a wild beast in just your undergarments."

Alistair smirked, a little pleased he had a story about him. Then again, so did all the other knights. "It was just a boar. Is it true you slew a dragon for your knighting?"

Kythe shrugged his shoulders. "More like an oversized lizard."

So the bards told fibs. Although dragon did sound better than oversized lizard.

"What are you doing here?" Alistair asked.

"Participating in the tournament, what else?"

Alistair frowned. "But I heard you were married."

"Not yet, but I do have someone I want to marry."

"Then?"

"What? Can't I want to be king?"

"Not unless you marry the princess."

"I know," Kythe said. "I don't intend to win."

"Just here for sport then?"

Kythe shook his head. "Not quite. I may not want to be king, but I also don't want to have someone who isn't worthy sit on the Rowanark throne."

Alistair nodded. The point was driven home when he looked out to the crowd and spotted Destrian.

"Hopefully," Alistair said, "you'll see me fit."

Kythe winked. "We'll see."

Alistair smiled. It was good to see Kythe again. He should've gone to see him sooner. He didn't like most of the knights, but Kythe was an exception.

The chatter died down as King Hayden emerged from the keep. With him was Queen Ursula and Princess Leera.

King Hayden raised his hands and the ward grew silent. Even standing in the back, Alistair could see the king wasn't well. His royal robes hung off his boney shoulders and his eyes were sunken. His face was drawn, his skin pale. As a page, Alistair thought King Hayden was a giant, but this was nowhere near the man Alistair remembered.

Hayden surveyed the crowd and then began his welcoming speech. "I want to thank you all for coming—lords, knights, friends, and family. Within a week marks the start of the first ever Rowanark Tournament. I see many familiar faces here. Faces of the young pages who were brought from their fiefdoms to Rowan to learn and train to become part of noble society. I am happy to see how much you've grown. I have heard many tales of all your exploits and of the quests you have completed. I am proud to have each of you here once again gathered in Rowanark Castle where your new test begins.

"Each of you will be competing in the tournament as knights. The winner will have my daughter's hand in marriage and will become future King of Rowanark. This test will be the hardest you have ever encountered. It will determine the fate of Rowanark's future. You all have one week to prepare. Gather your armor, prepare your horses. Do not rest during these seven days. Train hard. Know your competition. You see them as friends now, but realize that they are your competitors and one of them, your future king.

"I bless you all and wish you all good—"

King Hayden coughed softly into his fist and cleared his throat. He opened his mouth to speak when he started coughing again, a fierce, hacking cough that doubled him over. He spat blood on the keep's stone steps. A gasp came from the crowd. Leera's eyes widened and she went to her father, her hand on his back. Her crestfallen expression left a gaping hole in Alistair's chest. With her father's arm around her shoulder, Leera escorted Hayden back into the keep.

"Apologies, my fellow lords and knights," Queen Ursula said, trying to maintain a calm demeanor. "The king is unwell and requires rest. The castle is your home. Arrangements have been made for each knight to have his own room. Welcome to Rowanark Castle."

There was some applause but it quickly settled. The nobles began to exit the ward. Alistair, Reynard, and Kythe, along with Kythe's herald, a tall, thin man, followed the procession.

Someone bumped into Alistair hard enough to knock him off his feet. He fell, and his plated armor pierced his back. "Watch where you're going, you damned ass!"

A knight stopped and turned around, scowling at Alistair. He was a giant, thick across the shoulders and down the arms, with a bushy black beard down to his chest.

With Kythe's help, Alistair got back on his feet.

"Careful," Kythe said. "That's Brom."

Destrian's younger brother. But he looked much older and was nearly twice the size of Destrian. Where Destrian looked like a delicate dandy, Brom looked like he'd been raised by a pack of bears.

"I know exactly who he is." Alistair glared up at Brom. His size wouldn't intimidate him. Brom's push had been no accident. A small group of knights circled them.

"You say something, little man?" Brom said, his voice like gravel.

"I said, watch where you're going."

"Oh, I'm sorry. I figured trash belongs on the ground."

Laughter. Destrian, standing next to his brother, smirked. Their laughter brought a flush to Alistair's face and heat raced through his body. They looked down at him even though he had the same noble blood as they had. So what if his fiefdom was more like a farming village than a high class city?

The page from Teerdock was back in Rowan, only this time Alistair wasn't a page. He was a knight and he knew how to defend himself.

"Think you're tough shit?"

That shut them up.

"Are you challenging me, boy?" Brom stepped toward Alistair.

"*Boy?* I'm older than you." To clarify, he glanced at Kythe. "I'm older than him, right?"

Kythe nodded. "By two years."

"How in the Great Depths is he this tall?" Destrian wasn't tall, neither was Norwood, their father. He'd never seen Destrian's mother, but she must be a wildebeest to produce Brom.

"I said, do you challenge me?" Brom was so close Alistair could feel Brom's hot breath on his face.

"Don't do it," Kythe said.

"Ignore him, Alistair," Reynard said.

Ignore him? Ha! This was the reason he'd come to Rowan, to show these stuck-up knights what he was capable of. Fear or doubt didn't play into it.

"You're damn right I challenge you," Alistair said.

Brom grinned, showing all his teeth, at least two of them made of wood. Something small in Alistair told him he'd made the wrong decision.

Too late now.

Destrian raised a fist in the air. "To the lists!"

Lists?

A cheer erupted in the air and before Alistair knew what was happening, he was on his horse, Hale, at one end of the list and Brom was on the other end. Brom's horse was a giant black destrier. Of course, it was massive—how else could it support Brom's weight? The poor horse's back must be in pain. Alistair would have to end this joust match quickly for the sake of the animal.

Joust. That was what he was about to do. The severity of the situation finally dawned on him.

"You look worried," Kythe said.

"He should be," Reynard said, a wooden lance supplied by the castle in his hand.

"Surely, you've done this before," Kythe said.

"Once or twice," Alistair said.

Hale shook underneath him, as if the horse could sense his growing doubt. He patted Hale's mane in long, smooth strokes. It wasn't like he didn't know how to joust. He understood the concept: charge forward, point your lance, and strike. He was an excellent rider and was trained in all weaponry, it was just that he hardly used it.

Kythe's eyes bugged out of his head. "Once or twice? Why did you want to compete?"

"We were to practice the week before the tournament," Reynard said.

"And you think a *week* of practice would see him fit enough to succeed?"

"He knows how to ride and he knows how to carry a lance," Reynard said. "He just doesn't know how to put two and two together."

"Actually, I'm not entirely sure what the rules are here," Alistair said. More doubt crept into his heart. Maybe he had been a bit too brash on this one. What was wrong with a duel? Why did it have to be a joust? Wouldn't they get enough of jousting in the following week?

"You realize what will happen if he loses," Kythe said, and he seemed the most worried of them all.

"I'm aware," Reynard said, passing Alistair the lance, "but it's too late now."

"What happens if I lose?" Alistair asked, taking the lance from Reynard. It wasn't heavy but its length made it awkward to hold. Seriously—what was so wrong about a duel with swords? Much easier, and he was good with the sword.

"You're not going to lose." Reynard's expression was stern,

serious. Well, he always had a serious look on his face, but this one had a sense of life or death to it. "Now listen carefully."

Kythe threw his hands up in the air. "This is absolutely insane. You're both insane."

"Jousters are allowed four lances and can run four courses per match," Reynard explained. "Points are awarded on a scale from one to three. One point for breaking a lance anywhere on the opponent from the waist up. Two points for knocking a helmet off. Three points for knocking the opponent off the horse."

As Alistair listened he watched his opponent on the other side of the list. He couldn't help but notice that Brom had more supporters than he had. Lackeys, not supporters. They joked and laughed and sniggered. These were the cruel lot who'd made his life as a page a living nightmare. Their nastiness echoed in his mind. Loser. Farm boy. Pig's shit. They hadn't grown up at all, hadn't matured.

Alistair could barely hear Reynard anymore. All the name calling and bullying screamed in his mind. He shook his head, trying to focus.

"If you hit the horse, you're disqualified."

Oh, I don't intend to hit the horse. Just the ass on top of it.

"Lances broken sideways…are you even listening to me?"

Alistair's narrowed his eyes at Brom. Maybe it was better he show what he was made of now instead of at the tournament. He'd put the fear of Teerdock into them all. "Point and hit. What's there to know?"

Another cackle from the far end. Alistair thought he heard the words, "Just like his father," uttered with derision.

All Alistair would need was to run one course. One course to smash Brom to the ground.

"It's not that simple," Reynard said. "You'll want to strike his side on an angle and push—"

Enough about the rules. Alistair shut the visor on his helmet and kicked his horse into a gallop.

"Hyah!"

"No!" Reynard called to him, but it was too late. Atop of Hale, Alistair surged forward, his lance pointed at Brom.

Brom charged ahead as well, and the sound of pounding hooves drowned out all the other noise and reverberated in Alistair's helmet.

They closed in on each other at incredible speeds. Alistair concentrated on the dragon emblazoned on Brom's breastplate, the Pendrakken coat of arms. His lance would break off that stupid dragon. He counted on it.

In less than three seconds, contact had been made—

And it had struck like a lightning bolt, fast and fierce Alistair didn't quite know what hit.

Or better yet, what hit him.

He lay on the ground, on his back. His helmet had rolled off his head. Cheers sounded. For him?

He lifted his head up and his vision swam. He spotted four horse legs and looked up to see Brom sitting on his destrier, the visor of his helmet up and a broken lance in his hand.

"Your armor and horse are mine," Brom said, and spat at Alistair.

Alistair dropped his head back down. He heard more mocking laughter before everything went black.

#

Alistair woke up in an unfamiliar bed within an unfamiliar room. His throat was dry and his head—by Cosima, his head felt like it'd been split open. A candle burned on a wooden table beside the bed. A window showed a darkened sky. The last thing he remembered was Brom standing over him, which meant only one thing: he hadn't won the joust.

Reynard sat in a chair by the corner of the room, his arms crossed over his chest, one leg crossed over the other. He had murder in his eyes. Disappointment, too, but mostly murder.

Alistair swallowed, and the act made his head hurt even more. His back and chest throbbed with pain at the slightest movement. "Where are we?"

"You're a damned fool."

He deserved that.

His room was a lot like the one he had as a page. Spare in furniture, but functional. His pack full of clothes and his sword lay on the stone floor, but that was it. "Where's my armor?"

"You lost it," Reynard said. "Along with the horse. Your father's horse and armor. Both gone."

"I don't understand."

Reynard rolled his eyes. "Obviously. You don't understand anything and you don't care to listen to me. I told you not to take that challenge."

"I couldn't just sit there and do nothing."

If it had been a sword match, he would've won. The sword was his strong suit.

"That's exactly what you should've done. Been the bigger man and walked away."

"I had to shut him up."

"And you failed. Miserably, might I add." Reynard stood up and went to the door. He opened it and loud, raucous voices could be heard. "You hear that?"

They were making fun of Alistair.

"They're enjoying a night of your misery. We only just got here and already you've managed to lose everything."

"But how does he get my armor and horse?"

Reynard closed the door. "If you challenge a knight to a joust, the loser forfeits his armor and horse."

"So I'll win it back in the tournament."

Reynard chuckled. "Two things, Alistair. One, the tournament is different with its own set of rules. It has only one prize, that being the crown. But a joust between two knights who follow the Knight's Code has different rules. And two, what are you going to compete with and on? You have no horse and no armor. Do you intend to jog on the lists?"

Alistair glared. "If I have to." He'd do whatever it took to win. "This is just a minor setback."

"Minor?" Reynard shook his head toward the ceiling, as if seeking advice from Cosima herself. "Even when knocked down from his high horse, he still has boundless amounts of arrogance."

"We still have a week," Alistair said. "We'll get new armor and a new horse."

"We have no choice," Reynard crossed his arms over his chest. "It'll be tricky, though."

"But doable."

Reynard had said it himself that Alistair was a quick learner. He already knew how to ride a horse into battle and use a lance, now he just had to brush up on his jousting skills. It wasn't like he'd never done it before, only that it hadn't been a daily practice for him.

Not a problem. He would learn, he would get better, and then he would win.

"But we have one other problem," Reynard said.

Of course, they did. Couldn't get any worse, though, could it?

"What?"

"We only have seven days to make you a knight." Reynard dug into his robe and pulled out a book. He tossed it, the book landing on Alistair's stomach with a painful thud. "Start by reading this."

Alistair read the title: *The Rules of a Joust.*

He agreed—a good book to start off with.

Chapter Five

Kythe snickered.

"You know," Alistair said, "you don't have to come with us if you don't want to, Sir Kythe."

"And miss this? Not on your life."

The morning sun blazed high in the cloudless sky. Alistair, Reynard and Kythe were making their way to the castle stables. Alistair had woken up early, with achy muscles. Every step he took sent a prickling of pain. It was mainly in his chest, where Brom's lance had hit him, and his back, where he'd fallen off his horse.

"Like you could get a horse from the king's royal stables," Kythe said.

"Trust me," Reynard said, who'd had the idea to borrow a horse from the king himself. Alistair figured they'd find a horse somewhere in the city. The problem was that it might not be a horse trained for jousting, unlike the king's horses.

"That's what I find most complexing." Kythe furrowed his brow. "Aren't you supposed to be the sane one, Sir Reynard?"

Alistair waved a hand dismissively. Was it insane to defend one's honour when a brute insulted it? So what if he didn't know *how* to defend that honour. "Ah, but you forget, my dear Sir Kythe, Reynard isn't just any ordinary knight. He squired for King Hayden himself."

Kythe's eyes bugged out. "Truly?"

"Helped the king defeat the Black Knight." Alistair stood straighter, proud that his knight-tutor had played such a crucial role in Rowanark's history.

"That's quite the knighting quest."

They walked across the inner ward where the list was set up for the tournament. Builders had begun constructing tiered seating out of wood. Rowan had the finest builders in the kingdom. It was why the castle and the city were so large. Rowanark Castle had to be. It was a symbol of power and authority. Some even claimed Rowan was the birthplace of Sar, the leader of the Twelve Knights, back when it was a small settlement. Of course, it wouldn't have been known as Rowan all those years ago.

"I didn't just help the king defeat the Black Knight," Reynard said, walking ahead of them. "I also groomed his horses. I spent a lot of time with the stable master. Don't worry. Getting a horse will be the least of our worries."

Alistair scratched the back of his neck. *So what are the most of our worries?*

"What was the Black Knight like?" Kythe asked.

"Fearsome," Reynard said. "All dressed in black."

No knight in their right mind wore black armor anymore. Gray armor was fine. Even a darker gray. But never pitch black.

"He could summon a blade made of black light, sharp enough to cut through steel like it was bread."

A blade of black light. That contrasted the Twelve Knights, who carried no weapons or armor on their persons. Rather, the Twelve Knights were said to have summoned armor and weapons from a flash of blinding white light.

Just fairy tales. Who'd ever heard of light cutting like steel?

"How did you manage to defeat him?" Kythe asked.

Alistair remembered how obsessed Kythe had been as a child with legends of the Twelve Knights of Old and history of the Black Knight. Seemed he hadn't grown out of it.

"It wasn't just me, remember?" Reynard said, an edge in his tone. "It was me *and* the king. And don't you forget that."

Kythe winced, as if he'd been jabbed in the stomach. "Right. Sorry I asked."

Alistair clamped a hand on Kythe's shoulder reassuringly. "I've tried. He'll never tell. He's a man of secrets."

"Shut up, Alistair."

Alistair saluted Reynard behind his back.

The stables stank of horse dung. With all the time he'd spent on farms, Alistair was used to the smell. Kythe wasn't. His nose wrinkled. Reynard seemed impervious to the stench. He was a man on a quest, checking out each horse in turn until he stopped at a black charger that snorted at him when he got too close.

"This one's beautiful," Reynard said.

Big, too. Its leg muscles were toned and thick. If Alistair was on this horse, he'd win the tournament for sure.

A stable boy, carrying a block of hay, walked by.

"Stable boy."

The boy gave Reynard a cocked eyebrow and a snarky look. Seemed like he didn't care for being called a stable boy, even if it was, in fact, his job. Threads of hay stuck to his tunic. He was thin, but stood like a man who thought he had more meat than bones.

"My name is Sir Reynard of Rowanark and this is Sir Alistar and Sir Kythe. We need a horse for the tournament and will be borrowing this horse."

"You can't take that horse," the stable boy said. He had a ratty voice.

Alistair pointed to a different horse. "How about that one?"

"Nope."

"That one?"

The stable boy shook his head.

"Then which horse can we have?" Alistair asked.

"None of them."

"So much for easy…" Kythe muttered.

Reynard frowned. "I don't understand. These horses can be used for the king. The tournament is the king's tournament and, therefore, I am sure he won't mind us using one of his horses."

Reynard's voice was shaky. A first for him. Did he doubt that the king would lend him a horse? First, the horse was for Alistair, not for Reynard. And second, what had Reynard done to piss off the king so much that it even carried over to the stable boys?

The stable boy narrowed his eyes. "The horses can be used for the king's tournament, but not by you or anyone associated with you." He spoke down to them, as if he were the king's right hand.

Reynard bristled. If Alistair didn't know any better, he'd think Reynard was going to wring the stable boy's neck. In all the years Alistair had known Reynard, he'd never spoken a word about what had happened to him after the Black Knight had been defeated.

He pulled on Reynard's sleeve. "Let's just go."

Reynard yanked his arm free and pointed a finger at the stable boy. "If it hadn't been for me, stable boy, you'd be enslaved by the Black Knight. In fact, you probably wouldn't be alive."

The stable boy blew air between his cheeks. "Oh, please. What did *you* do? Give the king his sword before he delivered the death blow? Come now. You were a squire. Don't pretend like you had anything to do with the fighting."

Reynard closed his hands into fists. "You know nothing of what happened."

The stable boy grunted. "I know the stories."

But were they the real stories? And why keep them hidden?

A wisp of movement caught Alistair's eyes. A woman dressed in white riding pants and brown boots, her blond hair tied back. Alistair smiled and couldn't believe his luck.

Leera was here, paying a visit to one of the horses. Probably her own.

"Where is the stable master?" Reynard asked.

"You're looking at him."

Reynard balked. "That can't be true."

Kythe elbowed Alistair. "I think we should cut our losses."

But Alistair's gaze focused on Leera as she took a brush and stroked her horse's mane. "Huh? Yeah, whatever." He started toward her. "Cut something."

"Alistair, where are you going?"

"I need to see a woman about a horse."

Kythe slapped his hip. "Oh, for Cosima's sake."

Alistair left Reynard to bicker with the stable boy.

Leera combed the horse, a gray charger with black dots all over him. She hummed a melody, something soft and nondescript. Probably something to calm the horse's nerves. Some of the horses that were trained for battle had more aggression than the average horse. If Leera's song didn't soothe the black-spotted charger, it sure did the trick for Alistair.

A tingle shuddered up his spine, though whether it was from her humming or from her sheer beauty, he didn't know. She had grown into a beautiful woman, but what made her beautiful wasn't her looks alone. No, it was the way she carried herself. Prideful, but not like the rest of the nobles with their noses in the air. She kept her face level, her expression stoic, as if she were taming the horse with her demeanor alone. She radiated strength, and Alistair wouldn't be surprised to see her on top of that horse and competing in the tournament herself.

"Planning to escape by horseback?" he said.

If he surprised her, she didn't show it. She wore a hint of a smile on her face. "Somehow I figured you'd be here."

"Whatever do you mean?" Alistair gave her an easy smile.

"I saw the joust yesterday. Though I almost missed it, given how fast it went."

Alistair suppressed the urge to wince, both at her words and at the memory of the lance breaking off his chest. "Brom got lucky."

Leera cocked an eyebrow. She hadn't quite turned to look at him. Her attention was on the charger. "Luck? Or lack of skill?"

"Why can't it be both?" Alistair wasn't about to admit defeat, though he couldn't exactly say he was a highly skilled jouster.

The arguing between Reynard and the stable boy grew to a shouting match. Leera turned her head at the commotion. "Having trouble stealing a horse?"

"Borrowing, actually. And, yes, seems like Reynard's reputation is getting the best of him."

Leera's eyes widened. "That's Reynard?"

Alistair nodded. "Why the interest?"

"Mother has spoken about him a few times. Father never does, but they knew each other. Back when father was just a prince. They were friends."

"Unfortunately, it doesn't seem like that's the case anymore." He'd need to ask Reynard why, but would he get an answer? Probably not. "Looks like I'll have to get a horse someplace else."

"Too bad the tournament is jousting and not capturing the flag."

If she thought he'd forget what she meant by capture the flag, she was wrong. Not a day went by that he didn't think about that time when he was fourteen years old, days away from graduating from page to squire, and he had run into Leera, holding a white flag in his hand. Capture the flag had been the game all the pages played. It taught war tactics of a sort and encouraged a healthy competition between the pages. But when Alistair had found Leera, she'd been attempting her first escape. Alistair had forgotten all about the game and wanted nothing more than to help her get away from the castle, and, most of all, leave with her.

But before they'd gotten far, the other pages, Alistair's so-called peers, had caught them, and they weren't pleased that Alistair, the page from Teerdock of all places, was with Leera.

"That was the best and worst day of my life," Alistair said. Best because he had met Leera for the first time, worst because he'd learned then how cruel the nobles were.

Alistair approached the horse. "This is a fine horse. Yours?" He extended his hand out to the horse.

"Careful!"

The horse's mouth opened, its yellow teeth snapping at Alistair.

Alistair jumped back. "Whoa!"

The horse bit air, and thank Cosima for that.

"His name is Snapper," Leera said, playfully. That hint of a smile grew.

"For obvious reasons." He'd almost lost his hand, and that was not something Alistair could get back in time for the tournament. Or ever.

"He's a good boy. Aren't you Snapper?"

A good boy? More like an overly protective pet. "Takes kindly to you."

"And to anyone I tell him to." Leera caressed Snapper's muzzle. "He's a warhorse."

"What does a princess need with a warhorse?"

"I'm not all pretty dresses and shiny hair." Mischief gleamed in her eye.

Alistair weighed her remarks and added, "You smell good, too."

"Snapper's trained in the joust. He just needs a good rider."

"The joust." Alistair rubbed his chin. "And, pray tell, what does the lady think of the tournament?"

She couldn't possibly endorse it. It wasn't like the tournament was her idea. Her father had decreed it and so it was. She had changed in the years since they'd been apart, but if there was one thing he knew about her, it was how much she valued her autonomy.

That was the most attractive thing about her. It drew him to her, because he was the same.

"It's a necessary part of choosing the next heir to the throne."

Not the answer he expected. It couldn't be true. She toyed with him. "Really? The crown goes to the man with the biggest lance?"

"It's really about breaking the lance. You should learn that before you hit the lists again."

"I've been catching up on my reading." He'd read through the rules this morning before they all left for the stables. Now he had to learn how to win.

"You only have a week."

Alistair waved it off. "Plenty of time."

"You're that confident?"

Alistair pulled his shoulders back, puffing his chest out. "I am a knight."

Snapper grunted, as if he could understand Alistair and didn't believe his words. Alistair narrowed his eyes at the horse. The damn beast was out to get him.

"So are the rest. And they live up to their duties as knights."

"Just as you live up to your duties as a princess?" Alistair tested his luck by stepping closer to Leera. Snapper didn't try to bite him this time. "I remember a girl who wanted to do whatever she wanted to do. Now you're telling me you'll marry whoever wins the tournament?"

"It's my duty as princess. Whoever wins the tournament would make a fine king."

"Oh? And what if Brom wins?"

Leera blanched. Alistair leaned in closer to her.

"Can you imagine him as king? As your *husband*? You'd have to go to bed every night with that oaf and his wooden teeth."

She whirled on him, a blaze in her eyes. "How dare you talk about what goes on in my bed. Have you no manners?"

Alistair stepped back, his hands out in front of him. "Manners? Never had them. You forget. I hail from backwater Teerdock. I'm just a country knight. Where I come from, we don't have manners. We're no better than the animals we farm."

"You don't seem to be like that."

"Neither are the villagers." Alistair reached a tentative hand out to Snapper. When Snapper made no sudden moves, Alistair laid his hand on the horse's mane. For such a fearsome horse, its mane was delicate and soft, likely thanks to Leera's doting care. "But you wouldn't know that because you never see them."

"It's not like I wouldn't want to." Her voice was small, a little hurt.

"If I win the tournament, I promise you, I'll take you all over the kingdom."

He meant it, and that surprised him. Before this moment, he'd only wanted to show the other knights what he was made of. It never occurred to him to actually become king or marry the princess. Not until now. Not until he reminded himself of the girl Leera had been and the promises he, as a boy, had made to her.

It was the same promise.

"Do you think," Leera said, "the people would want to see me?"

Alistair nodded. "It's part of the reason I'm here."

"And the other part?"

"I hear the food's nice."

Leera laughed and the tension was broken. He liked the sound of her laugh. Even if he didn't win the tournament, he'd settle for becoming court jester just to make her laugh and hear the sound ring in his ears again and again.

"But I need a horse," Alistair said, "and I must say, I like Snapper's look."

"Why?"

"He's your horse, isn't he? He must be good luck." He ran his hand along the horse's strong neck. "What do you say? Think Snapper and I can get along?"

"With the right brushing technique, I think you and he will make fine friends by the day of the tournament."

Alistair smiled. "Perfect."

At least now he had a horse, and from the Princess of Rowanark no less. If that didn't mean good luck, he didn't know what luck was.

"No, Princess. He can't have him."

The words came from the stable boy, who stood with his arms crossed over his chest and shook his head from side to side. Reynard stood with him, a fiery glint in his eyes. If circumstances had been different, Alistair would've relished Reynard's frustration. As it turned out, in their current predicament, theirs was a shared frustration.

"These horses are for the king only," the stable boy said. "Your father would not allow Reynard to use Snapper."

The stable boy was irksome, to the say the least. He kept going on about the king's wishes, but acted like the King of Stables himself. And he still wasn't calling Reynard by his proper title.

"Well," Alistair said, "*Sir* Reynard won't be using him. I will."

"Nope."

"Can't you order him or something?" Alistair said to Leera.

"My father has enough to deal with."

Alistair nodded. He'd seen the king's condition firsthand. It wouldn't bode well for the king's health to cause a commotion within the castle.

"He can have him," a new voice boomed, and a stocky man with a bushy beard and eyebrows to match stepped forward. He looked older than Reynard, gray in the hair and with a leathery face. Moved like a bull, though, a testament to a lifetime of working in hard labor.

This was clearly the stable master Reynard had been hoping to find. Looked like he'd found them instead, and with perfect timing.

"And here they said you had retired, Guyon," Reynard said, shaking hands with the stable master.

"And leave the stables to these brats?" Guyon shook his head, chuckling. "Not on your life, old friend."

"It's good to see a friendly face."

"It's been too long."

Reynard nodded. "I've been meaning to remedy that, but you know—"

Guyon raised a hand. "I understand." He turned to Alistair. "If you want Snapper and the princess agrees, then you're welcome to him."

"But—" the stable boy said.

"And you." Guyon turned a wrathful glare to the boy, his tone menacing. Gone was the stable boy's bravado, leaving in its place fear and trembling. "If it wasn't for Sir Reynard, you'd be tending the Black Knight's dragons instead of these beautiful animals." The stable master slapped his forehead. "What am I saying? This castle wouldn't even be here. None of us would be. We'd be dead if it wasn't for the service this man did for our continued freedom."

Reynard shrugged. "I tried to tell him."

The stable boy lowered his head. "Yes, master."

"Now apologize."

"Master—"

"Apologize, or you'll be on horse manure duty for the rest of your life."

The stable boy winced. Given his scraps with Ollie, Alistair was all too familiar with manure duty. Not a fate he'd wish on anyone. Except Destrian, of course.

"I'm sorry," the stable boy said, not very loud, but loud enough for Reynard and Guyon to hear.

"And thank you for your service to the kingdom," Guyon added.

The stable boy looked at him, pleading with eyes that said enough was enough and hadn't he been chastised already?

"Say it," Guyon growled.

"And-thank-you-for-your-service-to-the-kingdom." He said it so fast the words mashed together.

"You're welcome," Reynard said, an amused curve to his lips.

With that put to rest, the stably boy retreated, leaving Reynard and Guyon to catch up.

"I promise I'll take good care of him," Alistair said to Leera.

"You'd better. And don't embarrass him by losing."

Snapper's ear twitched and he snorted, as if agreeing with Leera.

"Wouldn't dream of it. I'm scared he might bite my head off if I do."

Guyon lent Alistair a saddle and told him he could come grab his horse whenever he pleased, and that none of his workers would bother him henceforth.

"Nicely done," Alistair said to Reynard as they left the stables.

Reynard sighed relief. "One down, at least."

"What's next?"

"Armor."

Chapter Six

Alistair approached every blacksmith in the city marketplace and heard different variants of the word no.

"Make *you* armor?" That accompanied by a bitter cackle.

"You need it within the week? I can't do a rush job. I'm drowning in requests!"

"You're a knight?" Cocked eyebrow. "Never heard of you."

"I don't want to be associated with Teerdock." Should have guessed that one from the gold rings this blacksmith wore.

"Teerdock?" Genuine blank stare. "Where's that?"

Alistair plopped down on the steps which led to an inn. Either the blacksmiths were too busy or they didn't want to work with him because of his terrible loss to Brom. Word had spread too quickly. No doubt, Destrian, Brom and all their minions led the gossip.

"And here I thought hiring a blacksmith would be the easy part," Alistair said.

Reynard rubbed his chin. "I have an idea."

Alistair looked up at him. "You know someone?" He said it loud enough to be heard over a merchant yelling his wares. Something about buying two chickens and getting a quail for free.

"Yes, but," Reynard crossed his arms over his chest, "I was hoping we wouldn't have to resort to it."

Alistair swept his hands across him. "We've exhausted our options here. Where is he?"

"It's not a he. It's a she. And it's my sister."

Sister? Reynard had never mentioned having a sister before. Still, it was a clue to Reynard's life in Rowan. It must've been years since he'd seen his sister.

Hopefully, they missed each other and theirs had been a loving sibling relationship when he'd left.

Reynard led Alistair to an old house that looked out of place in this quarter of the city, which was neither poor nor rich. The house stood at two storeys made of mortar and brick with a pitched roof. It would've been a beautiful house if not for the broken windows and cracked facade. Or the empty wine bottles littering the front door.

"You grew up here?" Alistair asked.

The house looked abandoned.

Reynard frowned. "It used to be a lot nicer before."

"You sure your sister still lives here?"

A shout sounded from within. A man's voice. Something about drinking any damn time of the damn day that he damn well pleased, damn it!

Alistair raised an eyebrow. "A brother I don't know about?"

"My brother-in-law, Walter."

"Ah."

Reynard turned the knob on the front door and found it unlocked. They both walked inside. There was no point in knocking, since they wouldn't have been heard over all the yelling and screaming.

A pot-bellied man pointed and yelled at a woman who had the same sharp, hawk-like features as Reynard, but who was bigger in the shoulders and arms. She had long, dark reddish hair, and soot stained the apron she wore. Armor packed every corner of the house.

Breastplates, chainmail, greaves, shields, helmets, gauntlets. Even plated armor for horses. Alistair's jaw hung open as he took it all in. This place could arm a small army.

"If you would stop wasting your money on drink, we wouldn't be so poor," shouted Reynard's sister. Despite her biting tone to her husband, the dash of freckles on her cheeks softened her appearance.

"I'm spending money?" the man, who must've been Walter, said and waved around the house. Yellow stains marred his shirt and he carried a bottle in his hand, the contents of which spilled with each frantic movement. "Look at all these pieces of armor. You're not selling them. You just keeping buying material and making armor. I'm sick of it."

She worked on something while he yelled at her. Polishing the knuckles of a plated gauntlet. "Why don't you get a job? I loved you better when you were a traveling merchant."

"You want me to travel? Travel with what? I don't have a horse. I don't have a wagon. I certainly can't buy any of those things. We can barely afford food."

Reynard's sister shrugged a shoulder. "Got plenty of booze, though, I've noticed."

"Lovely family you have here," Alistair said to Reynard.

Both the husband and wife turned to them.

"Who in the Greatest Depths are you?" the husband said.

"Reynard?"

Reynard nodded. "Yes, Sybil. It's me. I've come back."

Reynard's sister, Sybil, left the gauntlet on the tabletop and went over to him. Her eyes searched every part of Reynard's face. "It is you." Her eyes lit up with recognition. "It's been years." Then her expression darkened. "Get out."

Alistair's jaw dropped.

Reynard frowned. "What?"

So much for a family reunion.

"Get out." Sybil turned her back to her brother. "And take your squire with you."

"Whoa," Alistair raised his hands, "I'm not his squire. I mean, I was. But I'm a knight. I'm here to enlist your help."

"You think I can help *you?*" Sybil said over her shoulder. She snorted. "Look at how I live. Now. Get. Out."

"What happened here?" Reynard asked.

Alistair smirked. Reynar and Sybil were equally stubborn forces. The quality must run in the family.

Sybil blew air between her cheeks and waved a hand dismissively. "Like you care." She sat back down and started polishing again.

"I left because I had to," Reynard said, stepping forward. "I didn't leave because I wanted to. What happened?" He indicated all the pieces cluttering the room. "Why are you making armor but not selling it?"

"Because no one will buy!" Walter said.

"Is that true?" Reynard asked.

"It's true." Sybil nodded. "And it's all your fault."

Reynard lowered his head and made no reply.

"You thought your actions would stay with you?" Sybil said. "You know what it's like to be the sister of the knight King Hayden banished from Rowanark Castle?"

"I didn't think anyone outside of the castle knew," Reynard said in a low voice.

Sybil slapped the cloth down on the desk and stood up. "Everybody knows!"

"Just want did you do?" Alistair asked. This was the second-time in a day Reynard's past had come up to thwart them. Maybe his father had made the wrong decision in Reynard accompanying Alistair. How much did his father know? Nothing had ever come up in Teerdock. Whatever Reynard had done, it had poisoned his sister's reputation, practically making her a leper.

"You didn't tell him?" Sybil snorted. She had a lot of bark. Maybe she should go up against Brom. "Typical. I bet you didn't tell anyone in Teerdock. That's where the king sent you, right? The farthest fiefdom in the kingdom. As far away from his wife as possible."

Alistair's eyes widened. *His wife?* You mean the queen?" The shock came at him like a lance to his breastplate. "No." Alistair shook his head. "You didn't. Tell me you didn't."

Reynard had been the king's squire, and he was the same age as Queen Ursula. No wonder the king wanted him as far from Rowanark as possible. But why hadn't King Hayden had Reynard executed if he'd interfered with his wife? He'd helped Hayden defeat the Black Knight, but was that enough?

"You don't know the full story," Reynard said.

Sybil came up to Reynard and jabbed her finger into his chest. "What I know is, you betrayed your king and your kingdom." Her husband stood behind her as if cheering her on by taking a swig of the bottle. The two, who had minutes before been yelling at each other, were now united in a front against Reynard. "You're lucky the king didn't kill you himself. Instead, he let you live in a fancy manor in the countryside. You left us without even a goodbye. You left us with a reputation that tarnished your family."

"Where's Mother and Father?"

"Dead, obviously. And because of you, no one wants to buy my armor."

"Dead?" His gaze fell, and his face clouded over. So much regret in just one word. "I'm sorry. I didn't think this would happen."

"You're not sorry." Sybil's eyes glistened, but a woman as strong as Sybil wouldn't let herself cry easily. "When was the last time you cared about this family? All you wanted was to be by the king's side.

Look where that got you. Now leave." She spat at him, her saliva hitting his shirt. "I don't want to see you for another decade."

She turned her back on him and went back to her work.

Reynard nodded and glanced at Alistair. "Let's go," he said, as he turned around and started his way to the front door.

"Wait," Alistair said, suspending what he'd heard about Reynard's past for a moment and focusing on the task at hand, "this armor is very well done."

"I know. Sybil was the best armorer."

"Still am!" Sybil called.

"We'll find our blacksmith somewhere else," Reynard said. "Maybe in Pendrakken."

"But that'll kill too much time."

"Let's go." Reynard's tone brooked no further argument.

Resignedly, Alistair followed Reynard. Before they made it to the door, Sybil and her husband started up on their arguing, right where they had left off. Something about money and one not being enough for the other. Alistair stopped and watched them. They reminded him of the fights his mother and father had. Not so much his father, who was never much of a yeller or an arguer and preferred quiet and peace to conflict. Even so, his reticence never stopped Alistair's mother from pointing an accusing finger at him and telling him that he wasn't good enough for her, not good enough to call himself a knight or a duke. That she ought to leave and find something better and never come back. She threatened every week to leave, but that was all it was, a threat.

Until it wasn't anymore, and Alistair woke up one morning to breakfast with just him and his father. And then lunch and then dinner. And every meal since then and after. Whether she found something better, Alistair would never know.

Alistair stepped toward Sybil and Walter. Their yelling was pointless.

The two of them were in each other's faces. A gruesome sight. They probably had loved each other at one point, before Reynard had done what he had and been sent away from Rowan.

"I swear to Cosima, woman!" Sybil's husband raised his hand to her.

Sybil steeled herself for the blow, but it never connected.

"Enough!" Alistair said as he gripped the husband's forearm in his hand. The man was bigger than Alistair in the stomach, but Alistair had strength through his chest and arms. Walter's arm shook, meeting Alistair's resistance, but did not budge.

Walter's face reddened. "Who in the Great Depths do you think you are?"

"A knight who won't hesitate to wring your neck if you so much as lay a finger on your wife."

With one movement, Alistair shoved him back and in his drunken state the husband fell back hard, crashing into a set of shields.

"She's my wife!" he said, as if Sybil were his property and he could do with her whatever he wanted.

"Exactly. She's your wife." Alistair nailed him down with a booted foot and put all his weight on it. "So respect her. Love her. Don't punish her because she's doing what she loves to do. What have you done? Get drunk and yell all day? How is that helping your situation? For Cosima's sake, man—do something with your life. Improve it. You have all this…stuff here. You're a merchant, aren't you? Well," he lifted his boot, "start selling."

"No one will buy," he said.

"Try harder. Get off the wine and get your ass in the market place."

Sybil had a smug look on her face, clearly pleased with Alistair's assessment.

"And you." Alistair turned his wrath to her and her face paled. "I don't know the real story behind what your brother did, but I know Reynard. He raised me and taught me to be a loyal, honourable knight. The man you're talking about, the man you're pointing fingers at, is not the man I know." He still had a lot to learn about Reynard, but for now, it could wait. "You want better for yourself? Then stop blaming others for your misfortune. You're a brilliant blacksmith. I can see it myself, and I'm sure others can, too. You must have had a damn good reputation before. You'll have it again, if you help me. Make me armor strong enough to win the tournament, and I promise, when I'm king, you'll regain the life you lost. What do you say?"

Alistair stuck his hand out. Sybil's lip trembled and then she glanced at Reynard.

"Don't look at him, look at me," Alistair said. "I'm the one you're working for. I'm the one who will pay you for the armor. And I'm the one who can lift you from this state."

"Pay?" Walter said. "Take it, honey. Whatever armor he needs, you make it."

"Shut up." Sybil looked down at Alistair's hand, then back up to his eyes. "If I help you, you'll see my reputation restored?"

"A knight's promise," he said.

"And if you lose, what then?"

"I'm not going to lose."

"But if."

Alistair licked his lips. "If I lose I will purchase all the armor you have lying around here."

Sybil's eyes widened. "What?"

"Alistair," Reynard said, behind him, "you'll lose your father's manor to pay for all this."

"Then we'll live in a mud hut."

"And what will you do with it?" Sybil asked.

"Probably build life-sized toy soldiers." Alistair shrugged. "What does it matter? Either way, you win. So, do we have a deal or not?"

She gripped his hand with her own. "We have a deal."

Chapter Seven

"Tell me again why we're here, of all places?" Alistair said.

Raucous laughter and angry shouts filled the tavern. The place stank of mead, wine, and, unfortunately, sweat, and was packed with mostly shady-looking men. These men weren't farmers or merchants. They looked more like criminals, thieves, gamblers, and bloodthirsty mercenaries. Reynard had brought Alistair to the poor quarter of Rowan located in the outskirts of the city, as far away from the castle as you could get while still within the city walls. They'd been there for not more than ten minutes, weaving through the crowds to the front of the bar, and already Alistair had witnessed two fights break out between table mates who probably weren't mates at all.

Alistair grimaced. "I'm sure there are nicer taverns in Rowan than this one."

"There are." Reynard looked the most out of place. Too much of a straight-laced noble. At least Alistair drank with the farmers in Teerdock, who sometimes got into their own fights when the night was late and the drinking heavy. "But we're not here to drink."

"I beg to differ." Alistair drank his mead and gagged. Nothing like the good stuff back home. "Cosima, it tastes like ashes."

"Then don't drink it." Reynard glanced around the tavern.

Someone bumped into Alistair from behind, then that someone

crashed down on the floor. The poor bastard had been punched in the face by a man with a shaved head. The man had only one ear, the other having been sliced or bitten off in some fight or as some punishment. He tossed his chin to Alistair, who had looked behind him to see what the heck was going on, as if goading Alistair to fight. Alistair didn't take the bait. The man had several others around his table, all brandishing an assortment of scars. As much as Alistair would've liked to punch the one-eared man's grin off his face, he didn't want to provoke something in this place which seemed to have its own rules.

He turned back to Reynard. "We're liable to get ourselves killed if we stay here too long." Alistair cursed under his breath. "Bunch of mercenaries here."

Reynard nodded. "It's where we'll find you a trainer."

"Trainer? From here?"

"Trust me."

"Why can't *you* train me? You did in the past. Albeit, begrudgingly."

"Considering my current predicament, it may be best if I remain hidden from the watchful gaze of Rowanark Castle."

Alistair rolled his eyes, and took another sip. Definitely an acquired taste. "So much for you being my herald."

"I didn't think it'd be this bad."

"Maybe next time you'll think twice before sleeping with the king's wife."

Reynard stared piercingly at Alistair. "You don't understand."

"Then tell me."

"I loved her."

The words were said with such truth that a chill ran down Alistair's spine. He'd never thought Reynard capable of love. Not his Reynard at least. His Reynard was stuck up, proud, one would even say void of emotion. But there was no doubting that Reynard truly did love the queen. His stare drilled into Alistair, his sky-blue eyes hardening. Something rested behind those eyes. Treasured memories that Reynard had kept locked away deep inside of himself.

But Alistair could've sworn he heard a pang of regret in Reynard's voice. As if something terrible had happened with his love for the queen.

Before Alistair could say anything, Reynard's eye caught something and he tapped Alistair on the shoulder. "There's our man."

"Who?" Alistair turned around.

A new face entered the tavern. A dirty, leathery face with a gray beard that reached down to the man's sternum. He looked like a big man, but it was hard to tell over the layers of rags he wore.

"That's our man?" Alistair said. "He's nothing but a beggar."

"I dare you to tell that to his face."

Alistair snickered. "Oh, come now."

The beggar dropped some coins from his soot-stained hands onto the bar top. The bartender surveyed the coins and shook his head. It wasn't enough for a meal, let alone a cup of the ash-tasting mead.

Without provocation, the bald, one-eared mercenary stood up with the rest of his cronies and approached the beggar. Judging by the smirks on their faces, their intention wasn't one of charity.

"That's not good," Alistair muttered.

The one-eared mercenary swept a hand and the beggar's coins went flying off the bar. The bastards exploded with laughter, then started picking at the beggars' rags, tossing insults at him.

Alistair gripped his cup so hard he could break it. The only thing Alistair hated more than himself being bullied was seeing someone else getting the same treatment. He knew exactly what it was like to be that beggar. Powerless to do anything, say anything.

Well, he wasn't powerless anymore. And he couldn't just sit there and do nothing.

He stood.

And sat right back down, Reynard's grip hauling him there. "Watch."

Watch what? The beggar become the laughingstock of the entire tavern? He'd be lucky if he left there alive.

The one-eared mercenary started pulling at the beggar's beard. His cronies surrounded him. Alistair thought he saw the glint of a knife in one of their hands.

One of the mercenaries put his hand on the beggar's shoulder, and what happened next came and went so quickly, Alistair almost missed it.

The beggar grabbed the mercenary's hand and in one swift motion, tossed the mercenary over his shoulder and slammed him down on the bar. Before any of the other mercenaries could react, the beggar threw a punch in one's face and a kick in another's stomach.

Three more were left, and even though they'd been unscathed so far, it didn't last. The beggar grabbed one of them by the head and pulled him down, the mercenary's nose meeting the beggar's knee. Blood squirted out in a crimson arc. A mercenary swept a fist across, but the beggar ducked just in time and countered with his own fist to the mercenary's chin, knocking him back and into a table.

The last mercenary drew a knife and charged him. The beggar stood there, waiting, then, in blur of movement, grabbed the mercenary by the wrist and kneed him in the groin. The other patrons made an ooh sound, as if the blow had been dealt to them. The mercenary dropped the knife and slid down to the floor, his face gone purple.

In less than two minutes, the band of mercenaries had been left moaning and in pain.

Reynard grinned. "See? What did I tell you?"

"I want him." Alistair pounded the bar with the palm of his hand. "Let's get our man a meal."

#

They sat in the corner of the tavern, the rest of the patrons giving them a wide berth, especially after having witnessed what short work the beggar had made of those mercenaries. Plates of chicken and beef, potatoes and steamed vegetables covered their table. Enough to feed a family, but it was all for one man.

His name was Konrad and he ate like a horse.

Konrad took a bite out of a chicken leg, chewed for a bit, then swallowed. "No," he said, and took another bite.

Alistair shook his head. "I haven't even…"

"I know who you are." Konrad's voice was gruff, low, yet it cut through the drowning cackles and rowdy talk. "I'm not an idiot." No, he wasn't. A trained killer, maybe, but no idiot. Had he been part of the king's army? Kicked out when the war against the Black Knight ended? "I know a knight when I see one. You want me to help you with the tournament."

"I saw you handle yourself," Alistair said. "You're a fighter. With your help, I can win the tournament."

"And I know exactly who you are, Konrad," Reynard said. Where Reynard looked like he could pass as Alistair's father, Konrad could pass as Alistair's grandfather. "You can teach Alistair techniques that no other knight knows of."

"True." Konrad shoved a potato in his mouth. "They don't make knights like they used to anymore."

Reynard grunted. "Tell me about it."

"Could probably teach you a thing or two as well." Konrad raised an eyebrow at Reynard. "Like how to keep it in your pants."

Alistair shook his head. "For the love of Cosima, Reynard, even the homeless know of your sullied reputation."

Reynard didn't miss a beat. "He and I are in the same boat, more or less."

Alistair scooted his chair closer to Konrad. "Listen, if you train me and teach me everything you know about how to win this joust, I'll make you rich. Sounds good, right? You'll never have to beg another day in your life. You can buy yourself a house with maids and manservants."

Konrad burped in Alistair's face. Not quite the reply he'd hoped for. The stench brought a new meaning to the term foul.

"I don't care for money. If I wanted riches I could rob a rich man."

Alistair had no doubt.

Konrad picked up a lamb chop and studied it, as if weighing whether to eat it or not. "I want to be a knight again," he said, before sinking his teeth into the meat.

Alistair frowned. "A knight again?"

"Konrad was stripped of his title as knight by the king," Reynard said.

"Why?"

"Because," Reynard leaned back in his seat, crossed his arms over his chest, and nodded toward Konrad, "he was a general in the Black Knight's army."

Alistair's blood ran cold. He darted looks from Reynard and Konrad. He was sitting with—no, *feeding*—someone who had ridden with the Black Knight. Who had killed men, women, and children. Whose war cry was rape and pillage. This man had razed village after village, town after town, city after city. He was no trainer, but a menace.

"Don't worry, boy." Konrad winked at him and flashed him his yellow-brownish teeth. "I won't bite you."

Alistair leaned toward Reynard. "You didn't tell me this." His voice hissed. "Are you mad? He's a danger to the kingdom."

"He's a poor beggar."

"I can hear you," Konrad said.

Alistair grabbed Reynard by the arm and hoisted him off his seat and out of earshot. "And you want me to train with him? What kind of techniques is he going to teach me? How to strangle children?"

"He's not an evil man."

Did Reynard hear himself speak? This was the reason they hardly got along. It was like they spoke different languages, grew up with different morals. "He worked for an evil man."

"Yes, he did. But the Black Knight had many on his side before he became known as the Black Knight. And by that time, anyone who even hinted at leaving his army was hunted and killed by the Black Knight himself, along with his family and all those he held dear. When you joined with the Black Knight, you forfeited your life."

"You're telling me he had no choice."

"I'm telling you that he's your best shot at winning," Reynard said. "He could best me in a fight."

Alistair looked at the killer stuffing his face. When he'd first seen him, he'd thought a breeze could push the man down. But looks were deceiving. "He'd sooner slit my throat."

Reynard gripped Alistair's shoulders. "Do you really think he'd slit your throat? You heard him. He could rob a rich man for all his worth, but has he? No. Has he murdered anyone? No. He made a mistake and he's suffering for it. He's lost everything. Now you can give him a chance to redeem himself."

Alistair rolled his eyes. "You make it sound so altruistic."

"It's not. You're not doing this out of the goodness of your heart. You're doing this to win."

Konrad should've been executed, but the king had left him stripped of land, money, and title, and of any way of getting back to a normal life again. In some ways, that was worse than death. He had to live in shame. And Reynard was right—Konrad could've mugged the wealthy. Probably could've made himself a half decent living, as long as he didn't get caught. But he chose not to. And he hadn't left Rowan, either. For all Alistair knew, the king had Konrad under careful watch and he couldn't leave. He was trapped, with no way of helping himself.

He needed Alistair as much as Alistair needed him. He didn't know what happened during the war on the Black Knight. Only what he'd read in history books. But those books had been written by the victor.

"I'll help him," Alistair said.

They went back to Konrad, who stood from his chair to meet them.

"If you train me and I win the tournament, I will reinstate your knighthood."

Konrad grinned.

"So, what do you say?"

"I agree. On one condition."

Alistair narrowed his eyes at him. "And that is?"

#

"All I have to do is hit you one time?" Alistair said.

"Yup," Konrad said, stretching his neck from side to side.

"What for?"

"If I'm going to train you, I need to know you're worthy of becoming a king. I'm not making a deal with a boy who's going to end up in last place."

Alistair squeezed his hands into fists. "I'm not going to end up in last place."

Konrad grinned. "Good."

Konrad had led Alistair and Reynard to the back alleyway of the tavern. A man laid passed out drunk—or at least, Alistair thought he was drunk—on the cobblestones. It was dark, except for the few lights pouring out from the tavern's back windows and the little moonlight that shined down from above. Farther down the alleyway, a man and women embraced each other, kissing. If it was just kissing, fine. Last thing Alistair needed was the cries of a woman or the grunts of a man on the cusp of an orgasm while he tried to land a punch on Konrad's cheek. Reynard and Konrad didn't seem to notice them, or chose to ignore the couple.

"Here's how it works." Konrad raised three fingers in the air. "Three rounds, and in each round you get three strikes. If you manage to hit me within the three rounds, you win, and I'll be your trainer. If you don't and your three rounds are up, you lose and I get a free meal."

"Is this a real thing?" Alistair asked Reynard, who stood behind him.

"It's a one-on-one melee," Reynard said.

"And you get three rounds, too?"

Konrad cracked his knuckles. "Yup."

"Who goes first?"

Konrad took off his rags, dropped them on the ground, and kicked them aside. Alistair's eyes widened at Konrad's muscled chest and bulging arms. For an old guy, he had not an ounce of fat on him. In the rags, he'd looked like any other old hunched-back beggar. Turned out that hunched back was pure power.

Alistair gulped.

Konrad took a fighting stance and gestured to him. "Ladies first."

"Ha, ha, very funny," Alistair said. He shook himself. So what if the old man had muscle? So he exercised—so what? Alistair had nothing to be worried about. Konrad was an elder, and old people didn't have all the faculties they once had at their disposal. Like speed.

Alistair smirked. He'd end this in one round.

He advanced on Konrad, fists held up. A knight was trained in all manner of combat, from the sword to the lance to the bow and arrow and even down to hands and feet. He launched an onslaught on Konrad, his fist flying. One, two, three—all missed.

For a big, old guy, Konrad moved like the wind. He ducked and side stepped each of Alistair's attacks. His eyes had been trained on Alistair's chest the whole time, focused.

With Alistair's first three attempts gone in a flash, his turn was over. Konrad showed all his teeth in a wide, almost maniacal grin. "My turn."

He sounded too happy about that. Alistair backed up. Was he afraid? No. That couldn't be it.

"So, tell me," Konrad said as he bounced toward Alistair, "why's a knight like you want to be king for?"

His fist came up, and would've nailed Alistair across the cheek if he hadn't ducked in time.

Phew. It hadn't been that bad. As long as he kept this up, he'd be fine. Thing was, the game was only over after either the three rounds were done or Alistair landed a hit. But Konrad could hit him as much as the three strikes permitted.

"Doesn't every noble want to be king someday?" Alistair said, trying to guess at Konrad's next attack.

"Nah. There's something you want."

"I want to rule."

Who talked during a fight?

The one who was confident he'd win, that was who.

"Guess again."

"Fine. Even with the Black Knight gone, there's still injustice in this kingdom. Particularly with the knights of today."

"True." Konrad nodded, or was that a way of distracting Alistair?

"You lot are nothing but snotty, spoiled brats."

Behind Alistair, Reynard lamented. "Truer words have never been spoken."

"I plan to put a stop to that," Alistair said.

"Valid. But there's more." Konrad threw a punch that caught Alistair off guard. He didn't have time to dodge it. He closed his eyes, bracing for the inevitable hit that would crush his cheek bone.

Seconds passed and no explosive pain. He opened his eyes.

Konrad's fist hovered over his cheek.

"Wouldn't want to ruin my future king's face, now would I?" Konrad said.

Alistair gave a withering chuckle, counting himself lucky. Then Konrad's fist slammed into his stomach. All the air in Alistair's lungs fled. He staggered back and almost collapsed before two arms lifted him up and kept him on his feet.

"Come on," Reynard said. "You can land *one* punch on him. He's older than me for Cosima's sake!"

"He's…a…fast…old bas..tard," Alistair said between gasps of air.

Reynard steadied him. "You're faster. Now go."

Round two. Alistair glared at Konrad. *Fun's over, you old fart.*

"You're right," Alistair said. He attacked and missed. "There is something more I want." Attack two, also a miss. "I want to prove to everyone I'm a great knight." Third attack?

Touched nothing but air.

"You'll have to do better than that," Konrad said.

Konrad's turn again.

Alistair didn't doubt it this time—he was scared. His stomach tensed as if remembering the last blow.

The first strike Alistair jumped back, Konrad's fist coming nowhere near him. He thought that a clever strategy until he realized that if he kept jumping back, sooner or later he'd either bump into

Reynard or stumble into the couple that was now, more or less, in the middle of coitus.

"You sure this ain't got nothing to do with marrying the princess?"

"Whatever do you mean?" Alistair played ignorant.

"Come now, Alistair. I've seen her. She's gorgeous. I'm sure every knight would kill for a chance to be under her bedsheets."

Konrad threw a punch and this time Alistair, instead of jumping back, leaned as far back as he could. The fist grazed his shirt. Then Alistair shoved Konrad, hard.

"Watch your tongue!" Alistair said. "That's the princess you're talking about."

"Oh?" Konrad cocked an eyebrow, clearly amused with Alistair's outburst "What are you going to do about it?"

Konrad kicked the ground with his boot, his heel skidding on the cobblestones, and dust shot up in the air and at Alistair. Alistair fanned the dust cloud at his face, coughing.

Before he was finished, Konrad's fist lanced into his ribs. He staggered back, but this time didn't need Reynard to catch him.

"That's cheating!" Alistair rubbed his side where the searing pain radiated.

"Is it?" Konrad crossed his arms. "There's no rules here. Just get as many hits as you can in any way you can."

"Unbelievable." Alistair spat, and thank Cosima it was too dark to tell if blood colored that spit. "Fine. You want to play dirty, I can play dirty."

Konrad took a stance, fists up. "Last round. Better make this one count."

Alistair balled his fists so tight he thought he'd break the skin in his palms. "I am going to hit you so hard the mercenaries are going to feel it."

Konrad slapped his cheek playfully. "Go on, then. Do it for your Princess Leera."

I can't wait to feel your jaw along my knuckles. He went for him and threw a punch and, like all the others, missed.

Instead of charging ahead, Alistair stalled. He needed a better plan of action. He couldn't just go in blindly, arms swinging. He'd tried that for two rounds and failed tragically. Konrad was too fast, too well trained. Alistair needed to trick him. But how? Kicking dust in the air was out of the question.

Kicking, though. All this time he'd believed he had to land a punch.

Maybe not.

But a kick was slow and clumsy. Konrad would see it well before Alistair struck. But what if he surprised him?

He had an idea, but he wasn't quite sure it would work. Either way, it was better than just throwing his fists around or standing there doing nothing.

With a roar, he surged after Konrad, fist raised. Konrad smirked at him, his eyes gleaming with eagerness. Alistair couldn't wait to see that smug look wiped off his face.

He swung his fist around, intending to smash Konrad's across the face. But Konrad expected it and ducked—

Which was exactly what Alistair wanted him to do.

He followed through with his punch, using the momentum to twist his body down and around, kicking his foot out and sweeping it across Konrad's feet.

His foot hooked on Konrad and the force of the spin knocked Konrad off his feet, causing him to crash down on his back and hit the cobblestones with an audible thunk.

"Ha!" Alistair said as he regained his footing. "Got you!"

The look of shock on Konrad's face was priceless. Alistair thanked

Cosima his plan worked. He held his hand out and helped Konrad back up.

"Well done," Konrad said.

"You'll train me?"

"I'll train you, and if you win…"

"I'll make you a knight again. You'll be head of my personal guard."

Konrad stared up at the moonlit sky. "Cosima," he said, "not even king yet and already he's got a personal guard."

"He dreams big," Reynard said, but his lips donned a smile.

"Tomorrow." Konrad slapped Alistair on the shoulder. "The Great Depths starts for you bright and early."

Alistair blinked. "The Great Depths?"

Konrad wiggled his eyebrows. "By the time I'm done with you it's going to feel like it."

Chapter Eight

"Fancy," Alistair said, as he walked into the castle's great hall with Reynard, both dressed in what Alistair called their noble wear—a finely designed doublet, woolen stockings and leather boots.

The great hall had been transformed into a dinner and dancing hall, with long tables pressed close to the floor-to-ceiling windows and an open space in the centre for dancing. In the corner of the hall, next to the stairs leading up to a platform that led to the rest of the keep, a music troupe set up their instruments. Torches burned in their sconces for heat and oil lamps glowed on the tabletops.

"We can't stay late," Reynard said. His long, gray hair was tied back. "Your training starts tomorrow."

Alistair winced. His ribs still hurt from when Konrad pummeled them with more than one well-placed punch. His feelings toward tomorrow's training were split: excitement and a little trepidation. Cosima only knew what that beggar had up his rags.

But if it made him as skilled as the Twelve Knights of Old, he'd be glad to suffer through it.

"You think I want to stick around here for long?" Alistair grunted. "This place reeks of self-indulgence."

"Have some gratitude. The king is throwing this for the knights. It's quite something."

All of the knights were in attendance. That meant Destrian and his brother, Brom, too. They sat by a table nearest to the platform, other knights crowded around them like flies to shit.

"Miss it?" Alistair poked Reynard with his elbow. "He probably threw parties like this all the time back when you were a knight in Rowanark Castle."

"He didn't. We were too busy winning a war to party." Reynard flashed him a mirthless smile. "Enjoy my sacrifice."

"Sure you should be here?"

"I'm here to make sure you don't make an ass of yourself."

"I'm perfectly capable of behaving," Alistair said, throwing a hand out in a lavish gesture and hitting a servant coming up behind him holding a plate of shrimp. The plate slipped from the servant's grip and crashed to the floor. The sound was spectacular. Everyone looked up. "Shit, I'm sorry." Alistair consoled the servant, who blanched. "Are you all right? It looked delicious."

Reynard shook his head at him.

Alistair shrugged. "He came right at me."

"Look, just behave yourself tonight. Before you do anything, think to yourself, would a gentleman do this? Do this for your father."

"I know. I'll be princely."

"Better than a prince. Act like a king."

Alistair caught a glimpse of Destrian and his motley of wayward knights chuckling. Probably at his expense. If only he was king, so he could say off with their heads. "And where will you be?"

"Around," Reynard said, "but mainly keeping to myself. Come find me if you need me."

"Right." What Reynard meant was that he'd be out of sight and out of mind. He could always hide behind the pillars. Hopefully, he wouldn't be mistaken for a servant.

Alistair found himself a table on the opposite side of the room from Destrian's. If he was to behave, then he needed to be as far away from his arch-nemesis, and the man's brother, as possible. Last thing he needed was to start a fight in the great hall at the king's own party.

Kythe slipped into the chair next to Alistair. "You look like a fine noble," he said, a wry curve to his lips.

"I can barely breathe in this thing." Unlike his armor, this outfit didn't belong to his father, but he'd grown out of it. He slid a finger under the collar and pulled at it. "This collar was made by a torturer."

Kythe chuckled. "Did you get everything you need for the tournament?"

"I did. Even a trainer."

"That you need."

Alistair gave him a narrowed eyed stare.

"What?" Kythe shrugged. "It's true."

Alistair grunted. Fine—it was true.

A new face entered the hall from the platform, one that burned in his mind and haunted his dreams every night.

Leera wore a dark red, silk gown that hugged her waist and flowed down to the floor. Her blond hair was tied up with a stylish pink veil. Jewels and gold glittered on her fingers, throat and ears. The dress exposed the curve of her neck, and her lips were painted a subtle shade of red.

"She is beautiful," Kythe said.

"She always was," Alistair said, more to himself than to Kythe.

"Seems she has a liking for you, too."

Alistair's cheeks flared with heat. "What would give you that impression?"

"Gossip from the stables. She gave you her horse. That's high praise."

"Who else knows?" Rumors could get him into trouble if they touched the wrong ears.

"Not a soul," Kythe said. "And no one will. I overheard the stable master saying something to his apprentice. You think I'd betray you to any of these other knights? Look at them. They think they're all Cosima's gift to the kingdom."

"Don't you?"

"I'm a knight. My duty is to the kingdom. If a war broke out, these knights wouldn't know the first thing about rallying for a battle."

"Neither do I," Alistair said, his words a blow to his pride. Yet they were true. Even if he became king, he wouldn't know the first thing about it. He barely knew what it meant to be a knight. He had knowledge from his time as a page and a squire, but books written by scholars and historians weren't real life. If he did become king, he would need Leera's help in the proper way to rule.

Kythe patted him on the arm. "Ah, but there's the difference. You know you wouldn't be ready. They don't. They think this tournament will make them fit to be king. They don't know hardship like Reynard or the king did."

"They made it so we never would."

Kythe nodded. "True. But there is unrest in Khasran."

Khasran was the land to the south of the Kingdom of Rowanark. Not quite a kingdom, more like several tribes and rulers fighting over land they believed was theirs. Rowanark had been much the same before the Black Knight and the united front against him. Rowanark barely had any dealings with Khasran, aside from the influx of a few families trying to find a new life for themselves in one of Rowanark's fiefdoms. Khasran had never dared touch Rowanark's borders. They had enough problems of their own.

Then again, the nearest border from Khasran to Rowanark was Teerdock.

"I'm going to go see Leera," Alistair said.

Kythe winked at him. "Good luck. I'm rooting for you."

Alistair shook his head. "Oh, grow up," he said with more cheer in his tone than he wanted. He left Kythe and strode toward Leera. She must have felt his gaze on her because she looked directly at him, but only for a second. Her stare dropped and a hint of a smile danced on her lips before she looked back up at him, rolling her shoulders back and lifting her chin.

Yes, she noticed him. What was more, Alistair could've sworn she wanted him to talk to her.

He was closing the gap between them when Brom shouldered into him.

"Recovered quick, didn't you?" Brom said.

Alistair kept his pace, his eyes on Leera. "I'm resilient."

Brom put his arm out, stopping Alistair, and stepped around to face him. "Dirt like you shouldn't be allowed to see the princess."

"Get your hand off me."

"Or what?" Brom's grip tightened on Alistair's shoulder. It ached but Alistair refused to show it.

He glanced over to where Reynard stood by a pillar watching him like a sentry. "You're lucky, Brom." He'd made a promise to Reynard and he wasn't about to break it now. Certainly not for an ogre like Brom. "You won't be so lucky come a week's time."

Brom tossed his head back and barked a laugh, letting go of Alistair and crossing his arms over his burly chest. "You think you have a shot against *me*? Please. I could break a lance off you blindfolded."

"We'll see about that." Alistair maneuvered around him but stopped cold.

The king and queen had joined Leera. His chance to speak to her had passed. She spared him a glance and shrugged her shoulders ever so slightly. He still could approach her, but he didn't want to bother

her while she was with her parents. He wasn't even sure if he could address the king and queen directly. They probably didn't know who he was, and any conversation about where he was from should be avoided. What if the king and queen were as unfavourable to Teerdock as the rest of the nobles? He couldn't take that chance.

Grinding his teeth, he spun on his heel and marched toward Reynard. He'd find another way to speak with her.

#

Leera watched Alistair walk away. He'd been coming right at her when that giant of a man—who would surely crush her if he won the tournament and became her husband—intercepted him.

Alistair looked handsome, too, and she wanted to get him closer. His blond hair shined with oil, the unruly strands pulled from his face. He'd even dressed up like—dare she say it—a proper king. She wondered what he looked like underneath his clothes and found herself not the least bit embarrassed by that thought. She'd never thought about another man like that before. Most of the men she saw were garbed in armor and chainmail from head to toe.

"You look beautiful, darling," Queen Ursula said.

"Thank you, Mother." She turned to her father. "How are you feeling?"

"Better," her father said, but his voice rasped. Subtle, but she caught it.

"He drank some honeyed wine with water and lemon," Ursula said. She wore a green gown with her hair draped down past her shoulders. "Seems to have cleared his lungs a bit."

"I haven't seen so many knights gathered in the castle in a long time," Hayden said, staring out from the platform. Leera got the feeling he was nervous about the whole thing. As if he'd have another coughing fit and be forced to excuse himself.

Ursula's eyes glittered. "Glorious, aren't they?"

"Tell me, Father," Leera hooked her arm around her father's, "who do you want to win the tournament?"

"Interesting question," Hayden said. "The man suitable enough to marry my daughter, of course."

Of course.

"Any particular knight in mind?"

"They are all worthy in their own way." Hayden folded a hand around Leera's. "But only one of them can steal my daughter's heart."

They shared knowing glance.

If only love could win the tournament.

"I prefer Destrian," Ursula said, and the words rattled Leera.

Leera rolled her eyes. "Yes, Mother, we know."

Her father chuckled softly.

"You should dance with him," Ursula said.

Leera blinked. "Dance with him? But no one else is dancing."

"So start something."

"It's not a bad idea," Hayden said. "Choose one knight to dance with. It'll start the dancing and would honour that knight."

"I get to choose?" Maybe this dancing thing wouldn't be so bad after all.

Hayden shrugged. "Why not? Choose the one you fancy the most. I'd be curious to know."

Yes, but would he be disappointed by her choice? Either way, her eyes went straight to Alistair. She couldn't imagine choosing any other knight. Definitely not Destrian.

Ursula clapped her hands together and addressed their guests.

"And now, my lords and ladies, the princess will dance with one of the chosen knights of the tournament."

What was her mother doing? Leera was supposed to choose, not her. Then Ursula gestured to her, as if to let her choose her knight. Leera opened her mouth, "I choose Al—"

"Destrian!" Ursula announced, loud enough to drown out her own daughter's voice. "Would you like to dance with the princess?"

Destrian stood up from his seat and bowed his head. "It would be my honour, my Queen."

Applause sounded by all except one knight, the knight she wanted most. Alistair. He looked at her with thinly veiled anger, though she knew that anger wasn't directed at her.

"Mother," Leera hissed. "I didn't want to dance with Destrian."

"There is no doubt in my mind that Destrian will win the tournament." Ursula clapped her hands together, a fake smile plastered on her lips. "You must learn to be with him and at least like him if you can't grow to love him. I'm doing this for you. You won't get a choice. Trust me, I know what that's like." She motioned to the band. "Music, please, players."

Destrian went up to the platform and held his hand out to Leera. "Milady."

Leera smiled politely and curtsied. She had no choice—again.

A soft melody played. But to her ears, it might as well have been a dirge.

#

Alistair stood with Reynard watching Leera dance with Destrian.

"Jealous?" Reynard asked.

"Don't get me started," Alistair said. He wanted to come off as neutral, as if this didn't bother him at all, even though he seethed inside. But his crossed arms and, doubtless, his scowling face, belied any hope he had of remaining unfazed. "I hope I go up against him on the first day of the tournament. After I unhorse his ass I'm going to get Snapper to bite his pretty boy head off."

"Easy now."

"What? I'm not doing it now. I'm still *behaving*." Despite the bitterness lacing his tone.

"Saw your run-in with Brom, too." Reynard nodded. "I'm impressed you didn't throw a fist."

"Honestly?" Alistair stretched side to side. "I'm still a little achy from my brawl with Konrad."

Reynard snorted.

This had been the queen's doing. She'd wanted Leera to dance with Destrian and had chosen for her. No doubt she favoured him as her chosen knight. What did the queen see in Destrian? Perhaps he was a good knight on parchment, but he wasn't right for Leera or for the kingdom. His demeanor wasn't suited as a ruler.

Alistair watched the queen as she smiled at her daughter dancing with the dandy knight. If only Alistair could speak with her, show her that he was just as good a knight as Destrian. Her eyes moved, scanning the spectators. It didn't take long for her gaze to fall on Alistair and Reynard.

Her gaze fixed on Reynard. Her face blanched. She looked like Reynard was the last person she had expected to see here, and yet there was a longing. The king had fled the platform. Another coughing fit? Alistair hadn't heard anything, but there was no doubt that King Hayden was unwell.

Alistair leaned into Reynard. "Why don't you go speak with the queen?"

"And get myself killed? No thanks."

"Did she love you as much as you loved her?"

"I like to think she did," Reynard said. "Obviously, it wasn't enough."

Reynard met the queen's eyes. If a conversation could be had through looks alone, this was it. Yet Alistair sensed fear in them both. Of something forbidden. Like they shouldn't even be in the same room together, let alone glance at each other.

Alistair caught sight of Destrian's hands sliding down to Leera's lower back. A little bit too low for comfort. What did he think this was? Alistair growled. He felt like a wolf on a leash.

He needed to talk to her. After this dance, who knew where she'd be? The festivities would start full throttle and she might get whisked away, playing the part of princess. He had to get her away from there. Not him personally. But devise a meeting spot for them where they could be alone and away from the crowds. If everyone in the castle was going to be in the great hall, then he and Leera would have to meet at a different part of the castle, somewhere safely hidden.

He knew just the place.

He waved his hand, making it seem like he yawned and stretched. The motion caught Leera's attention.

He pointed outside and mouthed the words, *To the stables. Meet me at the stables.*

She frowned at him, shaking her head.

He tried again. *Stables. I'll be there. You be there, too.*

She mouthed one single word, *What?*

Oh, for Cosima's sake, this had to have been one of the stupidest things he'd ever done, up there with that time he let all the farm animals out of the barn as a silly joke and it had cost him a whole evening trying to round up all the cattle and chickens back into their pens.

Thinking about that time sparked an idea. Things were about to get stupider.

He stomped his foot down like a horse, throwing his head back and shaking his hair side to side as if he was rearing back. If she couldn't read his lips, maybe she could read his actions.

It had the opposite effect. She looked even more confused, and a bit concerned, too.

He kept at it, throwing himself into the action, and let slip a whinny.

"What in all the Great Depths are you doing?" Reynard said.

Alistair stood straight, cleared his throat, then shrugged his shoulders. "Nothing."

#

Leera frowned as she danced with Destrian, looking behind him to Alistair acting like…Cosima knew what.

He tried to send her a message, that much she understood. Something about how he wanted to meet with her somewhere in private. But he conveyed his message like a man possessed. He looked ridiculous. Reynard chastised him.

"You smell phenomenal, Princess," Destrian said.

"Oh, thank you."

Destrian led the dance and she let herself follow his lead without thinking about her next step. She'd been so drawn in by Alistair's odd behavior that she'd hardly felt Destrian's hands on her until he spoke to her now. He had one hand in hers and the other hand on her back. He was closer to her than he'd ever been before and she didn't like it.

He smiled at her, an easy, confident smile. "Are you wearing that perfume I got you from Soniya?"

"Uh…" Who knew? She couldn't remember if she'd put on any perfume tonight, let alone a perfume Destrian had purchased for her. Soniya was known for its pricey fragrances, though. So maybe? She couldn't answer him that way, though, so she played the tactful, diplomatic princess.

She smiled. "Yes."

Alistair caught her eye. His bizarre movements started up again. He threw his head back then shook his head from side to side. He looked like he was about to sneeze. She mouthed to him, *Have you gone crazy?*

"Princess, is everything all right?" Destrian asked.

"Oh, yes. Everything's fine."

"I can't wait to win this tournament. Then we can dance like this every night."

"Right." Leera suppressed the urge to roll her eyes. "Wouldn't that be splendid?"

"Do you like to dance, Princess?"

My name is Leera. That was the thing about Alistair. He never called her by her title and always used the name her father had blessed her with, not the title she was born into. There wasn't anything inherently wrong with Destrian. Not really, anyway. He would probably make a good husband. But he wouldn't make a good husband *for her*. He just wasn't…her type.

But for some strange reason, that blundering idiot in the corner most certainly was.

"Very much so," Leera said to Destrian's question.

"Is there something bothering you?"

More than you know.

"No, no." She pulled him in closer. "Nothing at all. Just hold me."

"That I can do." He sounded like he'd been given a gift from on high. Now she could focus on Alistair without worrying about Destrian catching her expression. This song took forever to end and she wouldn't have been surprised if her mother made the band prolong the tune. At least it gave her time to figure out Alistair's cryptic message.

Meet him somewhere, but where?

Alistair dipped his head and stomped his foot. His shook his head as if snorting.

Why was he acting like a horse?

And then it struck her.

"Oh, the stables!" she said aloud.

Destrian pulled back. "Princess?"

"You're so…stable."

Destrian stood up straighter, as if he wasn't already. The man could teach school lessons on austerity. "Exercise, Princess. Daily exercise. And a balanced meal." He winked at her.

"Hm," she said. Behind Destrian's back she gave Alistair a nod.

#

Applause sounded when the dance was finally over. It had been the longest melody Alistair had ever endured. At least it had given him enough time to send his message to Leera. It had taken her some time to figure it out, and it had cost him his sanity in the eyes of Reynard, but now he had a place to meet with her and be with her in private.

Destrian stepped away from Leera and bowed, still holding her hand. He kissed it. She wore a tight smile on her face and yanked her hand away a little too quickly. Likely no one else noticed it as much as Alistair had. The other knights were too busy staring at Destrian with a mixture of awe and envy.

With the dance finished, Leera went back to her mother, shared a few words, and then slipped into the back. She shot Alistair a knowing glance before disappearing.

That was his cue.

Servants came out carrying plates of steaming meats and vegetables. The smell wafted to Alistair, and while he was hungry, he didn't want to miss his chance with Leera. He could always take what was leftover from the kitchen later. He excused himself from Reynard, making up some excuse that he forgot his handkerchief back in his room.

He fled out a side door leading to a hallway which led further into the keep. Windows spotted the hallway, looking out to a garden courtyard with stone statues half covered in vines. He started down the hallway.

A harsh coughing sounded. Alistair stopped. A man sat by the windowsill.

Not any man, but King Hayden himself. He coughed into a purple handkerchief.

"My liege, are you all right?" Alistair asked.

Hayden raised a finger, then coughed. It was brutal sounding. A cough that left one's lungs battered and scarred. Torchlight lit the corridor, and Alistair noticed blood stains on the handkerchief.

Hayden wiped his mouth and swallowed. "I was hoping no one would find me."

"I'll get you some water," Alistair said.

"No, it's all right. I just need to sit for a while."

Should he stay or should he go? Leera had likely reached the stables by now and waited for him. But the king hadn't given him leave, and it wasn't like he could say, *Sorry, my liege, but your daughter is waiting for me for a secret meeting.* Besides, he couldn't leave Hayden as he was. He wheezed with each breath.

Alistair leaned a shoulder against the stone wall. He could afford to be a little late.

"And who are you?" King Hayden asked. "Apologies. I can't remember every knight in the tournament."

"No apology necessary," Alistair said. "I haven't been back to Rowan since my days as a page. I'm Sir Alistair Rudell of Teerdock. My father is Sir Pydor."

"Ah, Sir Pydor," Hayden said. "Good man. Jolly. Always telling jokes."

"That's my father. Not the greatest knight in the kingdom."

Hayden's brow knitted together. "What makes you say that?"

"Have you seen him lately?" Alistair ballooned his cheeks and rubbed his belly. "Too much mead."

Hayden chuckled, and Alistair couldn't help but see the similarities between him and his daughter. They had the same soft, charming laugh, the kind that crinkled the eyes. "I suppose that was my fault. I never pushed him hard enough when we were all knights together. Still, he fought in the war against the Black Knight."

"He did?" Those were tales his father never shared with him. It was hard to believe that Pydor had been a knight when the king was, too. That they'd been friends growing up and had fought together and now ruled a kingdom together.

"Oh yes. Granted, he was more the comic relief in the group. But we needed that." Hayden looked out the window, though whether he saw the courtyard or relived memories was anyone's guess. "I needed that."

Alistair nodded. To think, his father, that round-bellied duke, had been part of the king's war party? He wouldn't have believed it if the king hadn't told him himself. When he got back to Teerdock he was going to have to sit his father down over a mug of mead and hear the stories.

Reynard was a part of that group, too, except that he'd been a squire at the time instead of a knight. He so badly wanted to ask about what had happened between King Hayden and Reynard, but asking was likely the quickest way to the gallows.

"You don't really look like him," Hayden said, narrowing his eyes at Alistair.

"I take after my mother's side of the family." The blond hair, the blue eyes, the arrogance, if truth be told.

"I'm glad to see Teerdock is represented in the tournament."

Alistair bowed his head. "Thank you, my lord."

"Is your father here?"

"Afraid not."

"I would've liked to have him here to cheer me up."

"Laughter is the best remedy?"

"Something like that."

Silence, except for the music playing from the great hall and the crickets sounding in the courtyard. Something niggled at Alistair, something he wanted to ask. It was about the tournament, a safer topic than Reynard.

"My lord," he said, "may I ask you something?"

"Of course."

"What are your thoughts on the tournament?"

Hayden cocked an eyebrow. "No one has ever asked me that. You know, it is *my* tournament."

"I know. But, and I mean no disrespect,"—maybe this wasn't as appropriate as he thought it was, but he'd gone too far already not to forge ahead—"it all seems a little…rushed."

"I suppose it is. I suppose it has to be." Hayden coughed again as if to prove his point.

"How do you feel about making your daughter marry the winner?" That was the real question Alistair wanted to ask.

"It's necessary. It's part of her duty as a princess."

"But she could end up married to someone she doesn't love." What kind of father would force his daughter to marry someone she wouldn't, deep down inside, want to marry?

Hayden adjusted himself on the sill. His gaze bore into Alistair, the light from the torches dancing against his eyes, making them flare. His jaw was set. Had Alistair said the wrong thing? Passed a boundary he wasn't supposed to?

Alistair swallowed, meeting the king's gaze. He wouldn't look away. It was as if the king were measuring his worth; as if Alistair had just asked the king for Leera's hand in marriage. In that moment, Hayden became the king he had been when he defeated the Black Knight and united the fiefdoms under the banner of one single kingdom. Gone was the frail old man.

"Then for her sake," Hayden said in a precise tone, "the knight she loves better win."

#

He was late and she was gone. The stables were empty except for the horses, Snapper among them, sleeping standing up, which used to fascinate Alistair as a child. He checked every corner of the stable and came up empty handed. Maybe she hadn't bothered to come at all? Maybe she read his message wrong? Maybe she waited long enough, cursed herself for being a fool, cursed him for making her wait, and left.

Damn it. Yet what could he have done? He'd have to explain to her what happened. Surely, she'd understand if he told her he'd been detained by her father.

He stepped out into the inner ward. A cool, welcoming breeze whispered through his hair. Torch and oil light flickered from the windows in the keep and different wings of the castle. It was here, in the inner ward, that the crowds would gather to watch the knights compete for the crown. He put his hand on the tilt, felt the smooth wooden surface of the rail that ran the length of the course, separating the two riding jousters. Alistair would be training on it tomorrow with Konrad.

The king had called the tournament necessary. As necessary as it might be, Alistair prayed to Cosima that the winner was the knight Leera loved.

Did she love him? Probably not. That was silly to think, of course. It wasn't like he loved her. Though he'd like nothing more than to win the tournament to give him the chance to love her.

"It's impolite to leave a princess unattended," called a familiar voice.

Alistair turned around. Leera stood there with a wry smile. She looked radiant. Like moonlight in human form.

"It's more than impolite," he said. "It's downright unacceptable."

She came to meet him. It wasn't the stables like he'd intended, but it didn't matter. So long as they were somewhere together and he could talk to her and look at her without worrying about others judging them, it was enough. It could be a downpour, thunder roaring and lighting splitting the skies, and still he'd rather be nowhere else than here, getting soaked with her.

"I could've been stolen away by Khasran kidnappers and used for ransom," she quipped.

"If that had happened, I would've raised an army and come for you."

Alistair stepped toward her and she stepped toward him.

"And what army do you have?"

"I've got my farmers back in Teerdock. We'll come to your rescue."

They were closer now. Close enough to make out the hay sticking on the tail of her gown, but not close enough to smell the sweet fragrance of her hair or touch her milky skin.

"Armed with pitchforks?" she said.

Alistair nodded. "And riding pigs."

She giggled, and a jolt ran down his spine. "A shame I wasn't kidnapped. I would very much like to have seen that."

"I like what you've done with your hair." He was close enough, and dared enough, to reach out and slip his fingers between strands of her blond hair. Part of it was braided, while other strands were left loose. "Or did one of your ladies do that for you?"

"It's of my design," she said. "Staying cooped up in the castle all day, boredom strikes and then—"

"You find ways to style your hair."

"I'm glad you like it."

"I'm sure Destrian commented on it," Alistair said, with a less than kind tone, but not directed at her.

"He didn't. Didn't seem to notice."

"I don't blame him, given how close he was to you."

"Jealous?"

How could he not be?

"That depends. Did you like that dance?"

"He didn't step on my toes," she said.

But that wasn't a yes. *Not a no, either.*

"He's not who I would've danced with, had I a choice," Leera added.

"And who would you have chosen?" Alistair asked.

She tapped her nose and mischief colored her face. "I guess we'll never know."

Alistair closed whatever little space was between them and put his hands on her hips. He was taller than her, his lips to her forehead.

She gazed up at him, wide eyed. "What are you doing?"

"May I have this dance?" he asked.

"Dance? There's no music. What are we supposed to dance to?"

He held his hand out for her, keeping the other around her lower back. "Just trust me."

She did, taking his hand in hers, and they danced, him leading her through a song comprised of crickets, the breeze, and their rustling steps on the grass. They looked at each other at first, neither saying a word. He liked how close she was to him, the feel of her hand in his, of the curve of her back. It'd been a long time since he'd danced and he was careful not to step on her toes. His mother had taught him to dance, and it was the only good thing she ever did for him.

He hugged her, bringing her hand toward his chest. Their faces touched and the smell of her hair consumed him. He closed his eyes and breathed her in.

In that moment, any doubts he may have had about the tournament, vanished. He wanted this to last for the rest of his life. He would fight for it, and he would win.

He had to.

Time passed, and they still danced. It seemed like only seconds, but it was likely several minutes. More than a single song. More like three or four. And yet neither of them broke away.

"You know what would make this even better?" Leera whispered in his ear.

"What?"

"Music."

Alistair, with his eyes still closed, began to hum a melody, making it up on the spot. He felt Leera's cheek tighten and knew, without a shred of doubt, she was smiling.

Chapter Nine

The morning weather was unforgiving. Dark clouds had moved in overnight and covered the skies, blotting out the sun. Heavy rains fell, splashing on Alistair's armor and helmet, a spare set he'd gotten from Sybil that, while not custom made for his body, fit him better than his father's armor had.

"A knight in the joust must have strength, speed, and accuracy," said Konrad. He wore a green cloak that Reynard had given him to counter the weather. The hood covered his head. "All three of these qualities must work together if you have any hope of besting your opponent."

"You want me to practice on the quintain?" Alistair said.

"Yup."

The quintain stood in the middle of the list. A wooden structure at the height of an average knight on horseback, it was t-shaped. One arm was fashioned into a shield, the target of Alistair's lance, while the other arm held a sandbag. Alistair couldn't remember the last time he'd seen a quintain, let alone practiced on one.

"You're kidding me," he said. "I'm not a squire."

Knights had gathered around them to watch, standing by the keep under canopies to shield them from the pouring rain. As always, they scorned Alistair from afar. He couldn't hear what they said but their mocking faces were much clearer than this morning's skies. Kythe was among them, but he stood several paces away, and he wore a pensive expression.

Konrad crossed his arms. "The Black Knight made all his knights train with the quintain."

Reynard nodded. "The king made us do the same. It keeps one's skills sharpened."

"Wouldn't it make more sense for me to go up against a real live opponent?" Alistair said. He had six days to train, and he couldn't waste time on a quintain.

"Maybe so," Reynard said. "But the last time we tried that, you ended up on your back."

Alistair glared at the gathered knights. One knight in particular: Brom. Destrian wasn't there with him, though. Probably still sleeping or maybe getting his nails filed.

"If you can beat the quintain," Konrad said, "I'll mount a horse and we can start practicing different techniques. For now, though, let's see what you got."

Snapper stood a few paces away from Alistair. The stable master had him saddled and ready to go. Alistair approached the charger, and Snapper stepped away from him, snorting.

The knights laughed.

Konrad cocked an eyebrow. "Maybe we should train you on horseback riding."

"It's a new horse." Alistair grabbed the reins. Snapper snarled at him but didn't bite. That was progress, of a kind. He mounted, fitting his feet into the stirrups, and patted Snapper's mane. "We're not friends yet, but we will be, won't we, Snapper?"

The horse grunted in reply. Alistair took it as a good sign.

"Lance!" Konrad said, and a squire, not more than fifteen years old, dressed in a hood, rushed to Alistair, carrying a lance with some difficulty. He hoisted the lance up to Alistair and Alistair gripped it with one hand.

"Oh!" The head of the lance dipped a little, but he managed to get it under his control. It would've been a disaster if he'd dropped the lance. "It's heavier than I remember."

"That's because it's not like the lances used in tournaments. Those lances are hollow at the tip so they splinter when they strike an opponent's shield or armor. This is a war lance. Learn to control it and I promise you the jousting lance will be as light as a feather."

The lance was twelve feet long and all iron.

"You ready?" Konrad said.

Alistair nodded, his focus on the quintain. Reynard had had him practice on the quintain when he was a squire. He'd been good at it then. It couldn't have been that hard. This was just a way for Konrad to test Alistair's skills, give Konrad a base line from which to work from. "Let's do this."

"Then ride!" Konrad said, and slapped Snapper on the rear.

"Whoa!" Alistair cried.

The horse reared, kicked its legs out, and charged ahead at full speed. The point of the lance dipped and Alistair adjusted his position on the horse and strengthened his grip on the lance. He didn't have long before Snapper would reach the quintain. He lowered the lance, tucking it under his arm. He pushed every doubt from his mind, forgot about the knights watching him, about Reynard and Konrad, about the tournament and Rowanark. All that existed for him was Snapper, his lance, and his target, the red X marked on the centre of the quintain's shield.

He struck the wooden board from which the shield hung, missing the shield entirely. The quintain swung around and the sandbag slammed into his back. He pitched forward, dropped his lance, then gripped the reins with both hands. He tilted to the right, then to the left, and then balanced himself out.

At least he didn't fall.

The spectating knights erupted in laughter. Kythe ran a hand over his face, as if Alistair's training was too difficult to watch. Reynard shook his head and Konrad yelled, "Come back here and try it again!"

Damn it. He could've sworn he had pointed the lance directly on the shield. But he hadn't *hit* the shield, let alone hit the X. Maybe it was the rain as it splashed into his eyes or he wasn't used to Snapper's vicious galloping.

No, he couldn't blame it on the rain or the horse. It was all on him. He was out of practice.

He trotted back to the other end of the list, maneuvered Snapper around, took a fresh lance, and tried again.

This time he missed entirely.

"Again!" Konrad said.

He ran the course a third time. The lance hit the shield, but not in the centre, and he didn't ride Snapper fast enough. The quintain swung around struck him in the back, flinging him off his saddle.

More laughter broke out from the knights. Who needed a court jester when you had a knight who couldn't even beat an unmoving wooden post? Getting up from the wet, soggy ground while their laughter mocked him had to be one of the hardest things Alistair had ever had to do.

"Maybe you should cut your losses and go back to your farm!" one of the knights called.

"Maybe I should cut your damned face," Alistair said through gritted teeth.

"Easy," Konrad said. "Does a king lose his temper?"

"I'm sure he does," Alistair said, head bowed.

"Of course, he does." Konrad grabbed Alistair by the shoulders and shook him. Alistair looked up at Konrad's smiling face. "But never in front of his vassals. He might lose it with the queen, but she's there to listen to his ranting."

"What's your point?"

"My point is," Konrad tossed his bearded chin to the knights, "ignore those fools and focus on getting better and then you'll have a queen to rant angrily to all you like."

Alistair nodded. Konrad's point was well taken. He had to do this for Leera. More than the ranting, he had to get better at the joust so he could dance with Leera every night as he had last night. He'd hum a new melody for her and she'd curl up closer to him and he'd run his fingers through her hair as they swayed. He kept that image in his mind, let it ignite him, give him the strength to push forward and succeed.

"Good," Konrad said. "Now try again."

Alistair mounted Snapper once more and held his hand out for a lance.

He was getting used to its weight.

#

Leera sat by the windowsill in her father's chamber, looking out at the rain and down into the inner ward where Alistair practiced on the quintain. He kept missing the target or hitting the target in the wrong spot or charging too fast or not fast enough. He'd fallen a few times now, and each time it was like she'd fallen as well, and she flinched. It wasn't all his fault, though. Snapper hadn't gotten used to a new rider. Not only did Alistair have to hit the target precisely in the middle, but he also had to control a half wild horse like Snapper.

She smiled when he made lavish gestures at the two other men with him, one of them Reynard. He yelled something. No doubt he was frustrated, maybe a little irritated. If only he knew she watched him.

Alistair hadn't left her mind since last night. They had danced for a long while before breaking off and going their separate ways, both back to the party but in different entrances. No one seemed to notice they'd been gone. She'd stolen glances at him throughout the rest of the night, and he did the same, but neither spoke to the other. It was their own little secret, and she loved the thrill it gave her.

"You looked lovely dancing with Destrian last night," her mother said. Her father lay in the canopy bed and she sat beside him. He wasn't having a good day and coughed more than usual. "The two of you will make a handsome king and queen."

Ugh. Leera suppressed the urge to grimace. "It was just one dance, Mother," she said, unable to suppress the edge in her tone.

Alistair ran another course. Snapper pounded the ground, kicking up mud. Alistair lowered his lance and grazed the corner of the target. The quintain swung around and the sandbag smashed right into him. Thankfully, he managed to keep himself seated on the saddle.

"He dances well," Ursula said, still talking about Destrian.

"I've had better," Leera said.

"Oh? Who else have you danced with?"

Like she'd tell the truth. Instead, she said, "My father, the king, of course."

"Ha," Hayden said, "now I know you're joking. Have you seen your mother's mangled toes?"

"You couldn't call what your father does dancing," Ursula said.

Hayden clasped Ursula's hand. "I call it doing the stomp."

Leera laughed, but her heart twitched. She'd miss these morning talks she had with her father and mother. No one else saw them like this. Not knights, guards, nor servants. It was just the three of them, talking, joking, a little harmless banter. These were the times they were normal, like any old family, instead of the royal family.

"What kind of dance partner would you want, Leera?" Hayden asked her.

Leera raised an eyebrow at her father. His question had nothing to do with dancing. The deeper question was what kind of husband would she want, what qualities did her dream man have? But would it matter what answer she gave? She wouldn't get to choose, anyway. The tournament was about choosing the most fit king of Rowanark, not about choosing the most fit husband for Leera. Still, she knew who she wanted, and she watched him now, training to make sure he was fit enough for both king and husband.

"He'd be charming," she said, "and always know how to make me laugh."

"Any magic tricks?" Hayden said.

"No, Father. No one could take that away from you. He'd treat me like an equal. We'd rule Rowanark together."

"How would you do that?" Hayden asked.

Leera sighed, thinking on it. "Well, none of the knights truly know how to rule a kingdom. They may have some experience in governing a fiefdom, but most of these knights have been out questing, not ruling. At least I've been here, Father, shadowing you as you've done your duty as king to your kingdom." She gave her father a sideways glance. "I'd say I'm more fit to rule than they are."

Hayden cocked an eyebrow. "The knights are trained for war times."

"And I know nothing of war or battle or swinging a sword. So should our peace end, that's when the king will take over."

"King and Queen sharing responsibilities of the kingdom." Hayden pursed his lips, considering. He smacked his lips together with a loud pop. "I like it." He turned to Ursula. "We do that now, don't we, sweetheart?"

Ursula tapped his hand reassuringly.

"What else does this champion knight have?"

"He'd be strong," Leera continued, looking down at Alistair. "Not just in body but in mind and spirit. Determined, too."

"I'm starting to think this man has no faults."

"Oh, Father, he has faults. He makes mistakes. He's only human." As if to prove that point, the sandbag hit Alistair again and this time knocked him off Snapper. Alistair jumped back up, his armor covered in mud, and walked Snapper back to the end of the tilt. "But he never lets his pride get in the way of improving himself. He refuses to give up."

"So he's stubborn," Ursula said, bitterness coloring her tone.

"In the best possible way," Leera said. Alistair mounted Snapper once more. He shut the visor on his helmet and stuck his hand out. A squire handed him a lance. "He'll do whatever it takes to win."

Alistair charged ahead, his back straight, one hand holding his lance, the other gripping the reins. Leera caught her breath. *He's going too fast. He won't make it.* He had to balance speed with accuracy. Snapper's hooves kicked mud into the air, his rain-soaked mane waving wildly, spraying rain water across the list.

As Alistair closed in on the quintain, he lowered his lance, aimed, and—

Crack! The lance slammed into the target's centre.

"Yes!" Leera said, jumping up.

"What's wrong?" Ursula said. "What's happened?"

"Oh." Leera bit her thumb. Excitement ran through her veins. "Nothing." Her cheerful tone belied that. "Everything is dandy."

From the window, she heard Alistair's joyful cry.

#

"Hold still," Sybil said, as she fitted Alistair with his custom-made breastplate.

"I am," Alistair said. Sybil tightened the straps and Alistair lost the air to his lungs. "A little looser please," he croaked. She pulled back the strap and Alistair sucked in a breath. "Ah, much better."

They were in Sybil's house the night before the tournament. Sybil had finished her part of their bargain by crafting a suit of armor made for Alistair. Now Alistair had to keep his side of the deal and win the tournament and give her reputation back.

His back was to the mirror, but he desperately wanted to see what the armor looked like. The process took longer than he thought. Sybil placed each piece of armor on him carefully, delicately, like she handled precious glass ornaments. Sybil's husband, Walter, sat on a chair. He looked sober with no redness in the face and, without the booze, he was more subdued, meaning he wasn't yelling at his wife.

Reynard paced around Alistair, his hands behind his back.

"How many courses in a single match?" Reynard said, testing Alistair.

"That's easy," Alistair said. "Four courses. Four lances."

"And what's the point system?"

"One point for splintering your lance. Two points for knocking off a helmet. Three points for knocking him off the horse."

"What do you get for missing?"

"A pissed off crowd."

"And if you hit the horse?"

Walter gasped. "Who would hit a horse? That's inhumane"

"Consider yourself disqualified," Alistair said.

"And if your opponent happens to drop their lance before contact?"

"I'll raise my own lance and not strike. A knight doesn't attack an unharmed opponent."

Reynard stopped in front of Alistair and nodded to him, the corner of his lip curving up.

Guess I passed his test. He'd trained everyday with Konrad, learning all of Konrad's techniques and tricky, but effective, moves. He'd even read through the whole rule book three times, cover to cover.

"I'd hit the bastard," Walter said. "If you're dumb enough to drop your lance, you're going to get hit."

"Shut up, Walter," Sybil said, though lovingly, with familiarity. She stood straight, took a breath, and smiled. "All done."

"Let's have a look," Alistair said and turned to the mirror.

He barely recognized himself, which was silly. He wasn't even wearing his helmet and so nothing had changed on his face. But the armor made him look like a new man. The breastplate curved over his chest with the Teerdock coat of arms, a wild boar, emblazoned on it. The greaves and gauntlets fit comfortably on his arms and legs. He moved side to side, checking all his angles. He looked ready for war, not just jousting.

More than anything, he looked like a knight. Noble, but not in the way he hated, not in the way he saw the other knights. He didn't look snobby or, as it were, on his high horse, but noble in the way he imagined his father had been—or Reynard or even the king—when they fought against the Black Knight.

All told, he looked gorgeous, and he didn't mind saying so himself.

"What do you think?" Sybil said, clasping her hands in front of her chest. This must have been the first time someone had worn her armor in a long time.

"It looks…majestic." Alistair rolled his shoulders. "It's so light and I can move about easily."

"That was Sybil's specialty as an armorer," Reynard said.

"It's fantastic. I feel like I could sleep in this thing."

Sybil laughed. "I'm glad you like it."

"But how…resistant is it?" Particularly to pain. The armor didn't feel like the other set he'd worn during his training.

"You doubt my work?" Sybil crossed her arms and cocked an eyebrow.

"It's just… I feel like a feather."

"Hm." Sybil grabbed her hammer and, without warning, swung it at Alistair, smashing into his breastplate. Caught off guard, Alistair fell back. Sybil stood over him, hammer resting on her shoulder. "Did you feel that?"

"Not a thing!" Alistair said. The blow almost tickled.

With Reynard's help, Alistair stood up. He ran a hand over the coat of arms. He hadn't asked Sybil to do that, but he was glad she had. It was a nice touch.

"I think I'm ready," Alistair said. He'd trained in the joust, he'd gotten Snapper to like him, and now he had a suit of armor. Only thing missing was an opponent.

"I know you are," Reynard said. "You've practiced hard. You've learned all that you need to succeed. And now you even look the part."

"I couldn't have done it without your help, Reynard. Thank you. And you, too, Sybil."

"What about me?" Walter said.

"How many pieces of armor did you sell today?" Alistair asked.

Walter shrugged. "I sold a helmet."

"That's worth a mug of mead in my book."

"Don't get him started," Sybil said.

Alistair faced the mirror once more. A week ago, he'd been a rusty knight, and now he was polished. "Tomorrow is the big day." He took a breath. "I wonder who my first opponent will be?"

Chapter Ten

Alistair had never seen a crowd so big.

The terraced seating built around the list formed a stadium within the castle's ward. Not a seat was left unattended. Nearly everyone in Rowan was there. But of course, there weren't enough seats. Those who didn't have seats could stand on the castle battlements, properly monitored by castle guards, and watch from over the balustrade, but still many hung around behind the seating to at least be part of the event, even if they couldn't see it. They'd hear the pounding horse hooves and the splintering lances. Nothing in the history of the Kingdom of Rowanark had ever taken place like this tournament and everyone wanted some piece of it.

Leading toward the list and the stadium, market stalls had been established selling finger foods, like charred meat chopped up and skewered with sticks, and drinks. One stall sold the coats of arms of fiefdoms sewn onto tunics or a knight's name sewn on the back. Alistair noticed a few people wearing those tunics, representing the knight and the fiefdom they cheered for. Another stand sold toy wooden swords and shields, and children raced across the ward pretending to be knights.

"Where's the coat of arms for Teerdock?" Alistair asked the merchant in charge of the stall. All of the other coats of arms were there but his own.

"Teerdock?" the merchant said, as he passed a tunic in exchange for coin. "That a fiefdom?"

"Yes," Alistair said. "In the far south."

The merchant frowned at him. "You sure?"

"Yes, I'm sure. I'm from there." Alistair pointed at the Teerdock coat of arms on his breastplate. "I'm the knight representing the fiefdom."

"And you are?"

"Sir Alistair Rudell. It's spelled A-L-I-S…are you getting this?"

"Sorry, Sir Alistair," said the merchant in a such a way that he didn't believe Alistair was any kind of sir, "but I'm rather busy at the moment."

"Oh, for Cosima's sake…"

The masses took his place in front of the stall. How could they forget him? Even if Teerdock was the farthest fiefdom in Rowanark, it was still part of the kingdom.

"Alistair!" Kythe called, waving a hand. "The knights are expected in the list."

And so it begins.

Alistair followed Kythe through an arched pathway under the terraced seating. He covered his eyes from the blazing sun above and surveyed the spectators. It was an awesome sight to behold. The sheer number of people seated to watch the tournament was more than the whole population of Teerdock.

"Magnificent, isn't it?" Reynard said. Konrad was there, too, his beard trimmed; still long but tidy. Knights were allowed a small entourage, usually a squire, trainer or herald. Most knights had squires with them, but Alistair had to make do with his criminal-turned-trainer and his knight-tutor-turned-herald.

"It is," Alistair said, his mouth agape. When was the last time the kingdom got together all as one like this? Other than the war, of course. If Alistair was king, he'd make the tournament a yearly event.

"Come," Reynard said. "King Hayden makes a speech."

The king, accompanied by Queen Ursula and Princess Leera, stood atop a terrace that reached higher than the others and was draped with tapestries showing the royal coat of arms, a lion with a twelve-pointed star above its head. Hayden lifted his hands up and slowly lowered them, the action silencing the storm of chatter. Not a sound could be heard over the occasional horse whinny. Only a king, loved and respected, could command with such ease and finality.

King Hayden prepared to make a speech and Alistair bit his lip. If another one of those coughing fits plagued the king, it wouldn't look good in front of his people. Leera sat in her high-backed chair with a concerned look in her eyes as she focused on her father.

"Welcome, everyone, to Castle Rowanark," King Hayden's voice boomed out to the crowd, "and thank you for attending the first Rowanark Tournament." Cheers and applause erupted. Hayden waited for the crowd to sober, a faint smile beaming out to them. So far so good. Whatever he'd done this morning, it had cleared out his lungs, at least enough to make this speech. "Today, and for the next six days following, you'll see knight pitted against knight in the joust. Each knight is trained for this event, and I have no doubt that those who stand before you will put on a good show. They compete for sport, but also for something more precious. Something that will determine the future of your kingdom."

Something caught in the king's throat. He cleared his throat and his hand went to his chest. Leera stood up and went to her father, draping a hand over his shoulder. Hayden patted Leera's hand and nodded to her as if to say he was fine and not to worry.

The look on her face said she couldn't help but worry.

"As you know," the king forged ahead, "the royal family does not have a son, a proper heir to the throne. I was blessed with a beautiful, courageous, and caring daughter, whom I love dearly, the greatest gift that Cosima could bestow." He smiled at Leera, and she smiled back at him, but she wouldn't leave his side. "But Rowanark needs a son. Our history has not always been a peaceful one. Wars have been fought and won to achieve the peace we now take for granted. I cannot tell you what may happen in the future of our kingdom, but what I can tell you is that I will do everything in my power to ensure the kingdom is in the right hands.

"Which brings me to this: I have decided that the winner of this tournament will be the next heir to the throne. He will have proven himself a strong, cunning knight. A man of noble birth through his parentage, and a man of the people through his service as a knight. He will be given my daughter's hand in marriage and will be crowned your next King of Rowanark."

The applause was deafening. All around Alistair, the knights roared and cheered and threw their fists in the air. Even Konrad got into it, raising both hands into the air like in a war cry. But Reynard was focused on the king, as was Alistair. King Hayden, with the help of Leera, took his seat. He sucked in air as if he'd been running instead of delivering a speech. Leera brought him something to drink.

Taking centre stage now was a herald in a robe and a pointed hat with a scroll in hand. He unrolled the scroll before him and explained the joust's rules and the tournament's structure. Matches would be held throughout the day for a total of seven days and four judges would determine the winner of each match based on the points scored in each course.

"And to start the tournament," the herald announced, "our first match of the day will be with Sir Alistair Rudell of Teerdock."

Alistair's chest sunk. Of course, he'd be jousting today, but he didn't think he'd be the first one. He stepped forward, some of the crowd applauding, and held his head high despite the nervousness running through him. Leera smiled and King Hayden winked at him. Maybe the king had arranged it this way, wanting to see the son of his old friend joust in the first round.

Very well. If that was his king's wish, then he wouldn't disappoint.

The question was: who was Alistair's opponent.

"Against," the herald said, "Sir Brom Vawdrey."

The crowd roared, making whatever they'd done for Alistair seem like a whisper. Brom stepped out of the gathered knights and bellowed savagely. Then he pointed at Alistair and, with an evil smile on his face, ran a finger across his throat.

"Round two, then," Reynard said.

Konrad gripped Alistair's shoulder. "Time to take your revenge."

Alistair nodded, then gulped.

The crowds cheered Brom's name repeatedly. It was clear who they wanted to win this match.

But Alistair couldn't let that happen. His hands shook and he squeezed them to fists. He'd have to go up against Brom eventually, why not go against him now? Brom may have beaten him easily the last time, but much had changed since then. At least, he hoped it had. Doubts wormed into his mind. It had only been a week of training. Was it enough?

He was about to find out.

"You okay?" Reynard asked.

"Yes."

"Not nervous?"

"Why would I be?"

"Why *should* he be, is more like it," Konrad said. "He's trained and ready for battle. You will not lose."

Alistair nodded. "Right."

"Then let's get you mounted."

The knights exited the list, leaving only Brom and his squire and Alistair with Reynard and Konrad at opposite ends of the list. The stable boys brought out their horses.

Alistair climbed up on the saddle. Brom mounted his own horse, a massive black destrier, bigger than Snapper. The horse was like its owner, a heavyweight beast. Both looked like they could crush a man easily.

Snapper snorted and reared back, waking Alistair from his dark thoughts. He shook the doubts from him. Even Snapper could sense his misgivings and that would never do.

He bent down to Snapper's ear and ran a hand over his mane, "Let's do this for Leera."

Snapper dipped his head and whinnied.

At least his horse was ready.

Konrad passed Alistair a lance and Alistair dropped the visor on his full helmet. Now he was ready, too, for better or worse.

His breathing rasped in the helmet. It was all he could hear. That, and his heart beating in his eardrums.

The herald lifted a flag and slashed it down.

Brom charged ahead. Alistair kicked his stirrups and galloped at full speed.

Now all he could hear was Snapper's hooves pounding on the ground.

Alistair lowered his lance as Brom lowered his. The distance between them closed and they crossed paths and—

Missed.

Neither lance had struck. The crowd booed. It was the worst start to a jousting tournament. They wanted to see lances splinter, chunks of wood and sticks fly out in every direction. They wanted to see knights fall off their horses. Instead what they got was a boring miss.

Alistair rounded the end of the list and waited. Brom kicked at his horse, as if he blamed it for his poor aim. Alistair glared. Few things in this world bothered him as much as animal cruelty. Seeing it now banished any nervousness he had. He couldn't wait to smash his lance into Brom.

The herald lifted the flag again and the second course began. When the two of them closed in, Alistair's lance missed, but Brom's struck Alistair in the breastplate.

Alistair leaned back, gripping the reins tighter with one hand. The lance grazed his shield and then splintered off Alistair's side. That counted for one point.

It should've hurt, but it didn't, thanks to Sybil's armor.

Cheers rolled across the list for Brom. With the crowd engaged, the herald wasted no time in raising the flag for the third course. A squire passed Alistair his lance and he galloped down the list.

Again, Brom smashed his lance into Alistair's shield, scoring another point.

It was two to nothing, and they had only one last course to run.

"Damn it!" Konrad said. "Focus!"

"I am!" Alistair said.

"Your head is up your horse's ass."

"Are you hurt?" Reynard asked.

"Not at all," Alistair said. "Sybil's armor is amazing."

"Then don't make this the only time you use it."

Alistair nodded. He looked over to the royal terrace. Despite the crowd's elation, King Hayden wore a deep frown, his eyes on Alistair. Leera bit her nail.

"This is the last course," Konrad said, passing Alistair his lance. "You can tie it and go to hand-to-hand combat or take him down."

Meaning, either knock his helmet off or knock him off his horse. No pressure.

Brom lifted the visor on his helmet. He grinned wildly and

pointed his lance at Alistair. "You're going down, Rudell!"

You haven't won yet.

Alistair had played recklessly. He had no strategy in mind. No target other than the big buffoon on the horse. Yet that wasn't the way Konrad had taught him. Konrad had told him which parts to hit for maximum effect.

The upper left of the breastplate—that was the spot. With enough torque, Brom would rotate to one side and be pushed backward. With enough strain on his grip to saddle and horse, he would fall. But the hit had to be precise. If the point of the lance edged too far, it would only glance off the armor and might not even break.

The herald lifted the flag and the fourth and final course began.

Alistair heard Snapper's hooves tearing through the ground, heard his own breathing in his helmet. His gaze zeroed in on his target, not just Brom but the part of Brom he needed to hit. He imagined it like a red X, the same mark the quintain had in the centre of its shield.

The mark grew larger. He lowered his lance, raised his shield.

He clenched his jaw.

He jabbed the lance into his target and it splintered. The side of Brom's lance smashed into him but didn't break.

He kept riding, tossed the remains of the lance, and pulled on the reins, turning Snapper around.

Brom threw his lance and gripped the reins with both hands, but he was too late. The momentum of the hit spun him around in his saddle and he slipped off his horse and crashed on to his back.

Silence. No one made a sound. Were they stunned in disbelief? Alistair took off his helmet. He had to admit, even he couldn't believe it.

The herald raised his hands. "The match is won, and Sir Alistair Rudell of Teerdock is the victor!"

The crowd roared, everyone jumping off their seats. It was the loudest cheer yet and now they called his name.

"Alistair! Alistair! Alistair!"

Alistair swung off Snapper and went over to Brom, towering over him. He smiled wryly. "Not bad for a country knight, eh?"

Brom's eyes were half open. His mouth hung agape. He lifted his head up, moaned, and went unconsciousness.

#

"You did superb today," said a knight Alistair had never met before.

"Thanks," Alistair said.

"Seriously, I didn't think it possible to unhorse a man the size of Brom."

Alistair rolled his right shoulder. "Still feeling it."

The knights gathered around Alistair all laughed as one. But he hadn't said it as a joke. Alistair's shoulder really did ache. Granted, the blow hadn't taken as much out of him as it had Brom.

To celebrate the tournament's opening day, the royal family held another party in the great hall. Celebrate was an understatement, though. The knights clinked glasses together and joked and barked with laughter. Before, everyone had been on edge, subdued, a proverbial lance up their behinds. Not so tonight. Of course, that only made sense, given that these knights had won their first day on the list and were that much closer to claiming the throne for themselves.

But only one would be left standing.

Right now, Alistair stood with several knights from the other fiefdoms. He didn't know them by name and hardly recognized their coats of arms stitched on their tunics. They chortled at whatever he said. He could be talking about milking a cow and they'd think he spun a legend of old.

"I'd better watch out for you," one of the knights said, winking at Alistair.

"I won't go easy," Alistair said, playing along.

Again, more laughter.

Alistair leaned toward Kythe who stood beside him. "What is happening?"

"They like you," Kythe said. "This is what fellow knights do instead of brooding in the corner."

"None of what I'm saying is a joke."

Kythe shrugged. "You've just knocked down one of the top competitors in this tournament. What did you think was going to happen? They fear you. Hope to get you on their good side."

"For when we joust?"

"Or maybe when you're king."

And then he could get vengeance on those who treated him poorly. Throw them in the dungeon! Lock 'em up in the stocks in the public square!

Maybe not. It sounded too petty.

"So why aren't *you* laughing?"

"You haven't beaten me yet," Kythe said.

Alistair raised his hands in supplication. "Excuse me, big bad jouster."

"They don't call me the dragon slayer for nothing."

Like Kythe, not every knight kissed up to him. Unlike Kythe, those knights wore undisguised hate on their scowling faces.

Destrian was one of them, and he had his own crew around him. He'd done well on his match. Too well. He unhorsed his opponent in the first course, and had made it seem easy. He was well trained, disciplined, and his aim was otherworldly. Worst of all, the crowd loved him the most out of the all the other knights. No doubt, they already viewed him as their champion.

His brother wasn't with him. Either Brom had taken an early trip back to Pendrakken or still recovered in bed. Probably the latter. It was odd that he even competed. Destrian would hardly let his brother win the tournament. Likely, the Pendrakken family plan had been to have Brom thin out the competition. Pendrakken would want to win the crown more than any other fiefdom. Pendrakken was as large a city as Rowan, and no doubt felt the most suited to rule the Kingdom of Rowanark.

Alistair smiled. Tossing a battle axe into their plan was almost as good as beating Brom to the ground.

The knights quieted as the royal family walked into their party, dressed in colored silks and brocaded tunics.

"I wonder who she'll dance with tonight," Kythe said.

"Who knows?" Alistair said. Destrian, if the queen had anything to say about it.

King Hayden stepped forward. He wasn't as pale as he'd been before. Maybe the excitement of the tournament did some good for his health. "Congratulations to all the knights who qualify for the next day of the tournament. You all competed bravely today. The crowd loved you. Even I got carried away with the excitement." He turned to Leera, her hair like gold, her eyes like the sea on a clear sunny day. "And, for the first song of the evening, my daughter will choose a knight to dance with. Choose your champion wisely, sweetheart."

Alistair's heart hammered against his ribcage. Would she choose him? Or had her mother already made her decision for her and this was just an elaborate ploy to make the knights *think* Leera had chosen one of them?

Leera stood beside her father. She surveyed the great hall, making a show of trying to find her knight. Then Destrian started to rise from his seat as if he'd already been chosen.

"I choose," Leera said, "Sir Alistair Rudell."

Destrian paused halfway out of his seat. The look on his face would have made the Black Knight quake in fear.

Alistair smiled, and had to struggle to keep it to just a smile.

"A fine choice, indeed," King Hayden said. "Sir Alistair."

Alistair approached the stairs. "Yes, my liege."

"I hope you dance as well as you joust."

"I won't disappoint."

The music began and Alistair extended his hand. Leera took it, and he escorted her to the centre of the dance floor. He wrapped one hand around her back and the other he held gently with his own.

They said nothing at first. Only gazing at each other, communicating with their eyes. Without words, Alistair told her that the dress she wore fit her perfectly, that he was glad she'd chosen him, that Snapper had been the greatest gift anyone had given to him, that every match he'd win in this tournament he'd do so in her honour, for her honour. At least, that was what he'd hoped the look in his eyes conveyed.

He didn't want to read too much into her look, but if he was a betting man, he'd bet his armor that she loved how she'd chosen who she wanted to choose and no one had done so for her.

"I have to agree with you," Alistair said, "this is much better with music. And an audience."

"Aren't you glad I chose you?"

"I'm on my high horse, that's for sure. But tell me something."

"What?"

"How pissed off does Destrian look?"

She laughed, and Alistair would've jousted a hundred Brom's to see that laugh again. She leaned over to the side to get a look at Destrian. "He's more than slightly miffed."

"As in?"

"Let's just say that if his eyes were crossbows, you'd have arrows sticking out from your back."

"Then I'd better bring you closer to protect me," Alistair said, and pulled her in.

"You did well today."

"Thank you."

"Were you scared?"

Alistair nodded. "Yes."

She probably expected him to say no, but that would be a lie, and he would not build this relationship on a lie.

"You were?"

"Have you *seen* Brom?"

She giggled. "I guess I should thank you?"

"For what?"

"I definitely didn't want to marry Brom."

"I don't blame you." One Pendrakken down, and only one more to go. "No matter what, Leera, I'm going to win."

"You keep saying that, but how can you be so sure? There are good knights here."

"There are." He'd seen it today for himself on the lists. More than a few of the knights would be a challenge. "But they'll all fall from their horses by my lance, I swear it."

"You're overly confident."

"I have to be." It was better than overly fearful.

"It's only been a week, Alistair. How could you know you want to marry me? You sound so sure of it."

"I am sure of it." He rubbed his thumb against Leera's hand.

"How? Why?"

"I've wanted you ever since I was a page playing escort to a princess."

Leera smiled. "That was one day. And you never did get me out of the castle."

"I know. I failed you then, but I won't fail you now."

"You must've had someone back in Teerdock."

"No one." He'd had a few relationships, but they had been short lived and swiftly forgotten. None of the girls he'd been with had made him feel as Leera did.

"Did you think about me?"

"I did. Though mostly I prayed."

Leera frowned. "Prayed?"

"That you wouldn't turn into a prissy princess in painted nails and fancy gowns."

She slapped him on the chest playfully. "Jerk." She paused, giving him a sideways glance, a hint of a smile on her lips. "And were your prayers answered?"

"In a way."

She glared at him, as expected. He had her right where he wanted her.

"You're not prissy," he said, "but I do love the way you look in a gown and your nails are pretty."

"I do them myself."

"I'm not surprised. I think that's what I'm drawn to most about you."

"That I paint my nails? Do my own hair?"

"Your independence."

She looked down at his chest and her cheeks grew rosy. "You're quite charming when you want to be."

"Courtship," Alistair said. "It's part of being a knight."

Leera smiled up at him. In truth, Reynard hadn't taught him anything about courting a lady, and while it was training for a knight, few knight-tutors trained their squire in love. Surprisingly, it came naturally to Alistair. But none of it was a tactic nor a trick. He said what he felt and truly believed.

Yet one question remained.

"But do you," Alistair asked, "want me to win this tournament?"

Her expression said everything, but she gave the slightest nod anyway.

When he was a page he'd wanted to kiss her, but had no idea how to do it and had been too embarrassed to even attempt it. Now that he was an adult, and she had chosen him as her champion for the night, he wanted nothing more than to feel her lips with his own.

This was a target he would not miss, and a hit he'd gladly fall into.

He leaned in and she closed her eyes. He licked his lips and she pursed her own.

Then the music stopped and applause sounded.

Leera's eyes snapped open. Alistair darted looks around him. They both had forgotten where they were.

He let her go and bowed slightly. "Thank you for the dance, Leera."

"No, thank you." She curtsied. "I hope we can do it again."

"If it pleases you."

She bit her lip. "It does." There was a hunger in her eyes he had not seen before. "Very much so."

Chapter Eleven

Alistair rammed his lance against his opponent's shield. The forceful blow pushed the knight so far back in his saddle that he looked as though he were lying down on the horse. Either way, it was impossible to keep balanced, and his opponent fell from his horse.

The crowd jumped from their seats and applauded, chanting Alistair's name. It was the third day of the tournament and there was nothing quite like the thousands cheering his name. With Snapper, Alistair cantered toward Reynard and Konrad. He waved to Leera as he passed the royal terrace.

He climbed down Snapper and passed the reins to the stable boy. "Take good care of him." He ran his hand along the horse's muzzle. "You did good today, buddy. Told you we'd make a great team."

Snapper snorted, and the stable boy took him away.

Konrad approached him with a big grin on his face.

"Not bad, right?" Alistair said.

"You were excellent," Konrad said. "Makes me want to compete."

"We're almost to the finals."

Konrad nodded. "Three more days. They won't be easy."

"I'm not worried." He hadn't even gotten close to losing. Brom had been his greatest challenge so far. The other knights he'd faced had been no match for him. He liked the joust, had a natural talent for it. If he'd known he'd be this good at it, he would've done it a lot more.

"Congratulations on your victory, Sir Alistair."

"And you as well, Sir Kythe."

Alistair hadn't seen Kythe joust yet. Kythe's matches usually happened after his own, while Alistair peeled off his armor and polished it. Still, he'd seen Kythe afterwards, and the man hardly broke a sweat. His matches didn't last long.

Destrian was the same. He'd unhorsed every opponent he'd come across. Alistair usually did, too, but sometimes he had to rely on scoring more points than his opponent. Still a victory, but the crowds loved a good unhorsing.

When the tournament was over, the inner ward became like a festival. This was Alistair's favorite time, not only because it meant he'd survived and won another day of the tournament, but because of all the attention that came his way. Children dressed in tunics with the Teerdock coat of arms sewn into them asked him dozens of questions about knighthood, all the quests he had done, and what it felt like to be in the joust. Men congratulated him and offered to buy him a drink, while their wives gave him seductive eyes.

He spotted Reynard and Konrad and excused himself from his loving fans.

"I could get used to this," he said to Reynard.

"Don't get too ahead of yourself." Reynard's lips were a thin line. "You haven't won the tournament yet."

"Oh, cut him some slack," Konrad said, a gleam in his eyes. "He's doing great. I've seen his competition. He has nothing to worry about. I trained him well."

"The other knights are trained well, too, and they've been doing this a lot longer than Alistair has."

"Reynard," Alistair said, "you worry too much."

A voice he cared little for called out to him from behind.

"I'm shocked you're still here," Destrian said.

Alistair turned to a mounted Destrian. "Scared?"

Destrian harrumphed. "If you don't become king you could always become my court jester."

"Don't you worry. I look forward to making you my chamber pot maid."

Destrian glared and rode away, his fans, and there were legion, following behind him. His nose was so far up in the air it was a wonder he could see ahead of him.

"Sir Alistair." A castle guard approached him, which was a first for him. Funny how anxiety washed over him at that moment, as if he'd done something wrong, which he hadn't.

"That's me," Alistair said with some caution.

"I bring word from the Princess Leera."

Alistair narrowed his eyes. Was this Leera's personal guard? No. She'd never had one before. The guard wore a full helm, too, covering his face. And gloves and boots and chainmail. Strands of blond hair peeked out from the helm. The guard also had a weirdly feminine voice that was—and he'd bet his life on it—strangely familiar.

Another one of Leera's disguises? She was good at it. If the whole princess thing failed, she might want to pick up stage acting.

"I'm all ears, soldier," Alistair said, humoring her.

"The princess congratulates you on your victory."

"Thank you."

The guard stepped closer to him, leaning in conspiratorially. "And she would like to meet with you."

Ah, so that was the reason for the disguise. "Where?"

"The dungeons."

Alistair cocked an eyebrow. "Dungeons?" Maybe he was in trouble after all.

"Trust her. She knows a thing or two about this castle."

Alistair nodded. "I'll be there."

The guard left and no one paid any attention to their exchange. Not even Reynard or Konrad. Nothing strange about a castle guard—garbed for war, practically—talking to one of the knights.

Alistair excused himself from the gathering and fled into the castle. He took the stairs leading down to the dungeons.

Other than being a little on the cold and dusty side, Leera was right—the dungeons were the best place to meet. The jail cells were empty. Not that Rowanark was crime-free, but it had jails in other parts of the city. No point in putting a thief within the castle. Likely the jail cells had been used during wartimes for war criminals, but that wasn't the case now. The only other negative was how pitch dark it was down there. He could hardly see in front of him.

But the positive far outweighed the negatives. It was private.

Just as his eyes began to adjust, a glow spread across the stone walls. It was Leera, carrying a candle in a gold handle.

"I liked your disguise," Alistair said.

A playful look danced on her face. "What disguise?"

Alistair went over to her with slow, calculated steps. She put the candle down on a wooden bench.

"You fought well," Leera said. Her chest rose and fell.

His did, too, with anticipation. "So your guard told me," he said, and closed the gap between them. He brushed his fingers along her slender waist. "She also told me something else."

"What's that?" she breathed, her eyes on his lips.

"That you liked to be kissed here." He brought his lips to her cheek and kissed her softly. "And here." He moved down to her neck and this time his kiss made a smacking sound. "And here." Finally, he kissed her right at the end of her nose.

She smiled. "That guard—she knows me so well. But there's one other spot I like to be kissed."

"Where?" He caressed her back with the tips of his fingers. "Do tell."

"Right here." And she kissed him on the lips. Just once, then pulled back. Her eyes widened and she was breathless. Alistair gazed into her eyes, at her partially opened mouth, at the curve of her neck. She'd kissed him. She'd made that choice for him. She had no duty to kiss him. She did it herself, through her own desires. She desired him.

And he desired her more than anything in his life.

This time, he kissed her, brought his mouth to hers and did not stop kissing her. He no longer touched her with just the tips of his fingers. He held her, pulled her to him. He touched her everywhere, as much as she touched him, as if this were the last time they'd be together. It was clumsy and urgent. It wasn't the delicate way one should kiss a princess.

But at this moment she wasn't a princess, she was a woman. His woman.

She broke away from him, her hands on his chest. "Should we be doing this?"

"Probably not."

"Do you want to stop?"

He smiled. What a question. As if he'd ever want to stop.

He answered with his lips and kissed her once more.

So what if this was wrong? It didn't feel that way. How could it be? It was the furthest thing from wrong. He was her champion.

But if he lost the tournament—what then?

No, he wouldn't lose. He couldn't. Especially now, knowing what he'd be missing, knowing what some other knight might have instead of him. She was his, and he was hers, and he would prove to everyone that they belonged together.

"Can we meet like this every day?" she asked.

"Absolutely."

#

Leera climbed the steps to her father's chamber. Her pulse raced and her heart galloped like Snapper galloped down the list with Alistair on his back.

Alistair. Just to say his name in her mind brought a smile to her lips. She touched her mouth and could still feel the tingling sensation of his lips on hers. She wanted to surrender every part of herself to him. He was a man she'd want to marry, want to call husband. If only her father would let her choose.

Maybe he would? If she convinced him that she'd found someone she loved, would he truly deny her that? Would Alistair make a good king? She had no evidence that he wouldn't. He treated her with fairness and compassion. Perhaps he'd treat his people the same.

She was in the hallway heading toward her father's room when she heard his hacking cough, a terrible, gruesome sound. She flinched, then picked up her pace and entered the chamber.

King Hayden was propped up in bed, his expression twisted as he coughed and spat blood on a handkerchief a servant held out to him. Leera ordered the servant to bring her father water. She sat by the bedside.

"Father," she said. He was having a bad day. No, this was worse than even his bad days. His face looked paler than usual and gaunt. A plate of untouched food rested on a tray next to the bed.

"Ah, Leera." He rested his head back. Beads of sweat covered his forehead.

"I'm here. Can I get you something?"

"I'm all right." He was anything but.

The joy Alistair had left her with moments before vanished. Tears stung her eyes, blurred her vision. She couldn't tell her father about Alistair, about how she felt about him and wanted to marry him.

That wasn't important now. At that moment, she hated the tournament. Yes, it had brought her Alistair, but she would've traded anything in the world to take away the pain and sickness her father felt.

Hayden reached out to her ear. His fingers slid over her earlobe, revealing a gold coin.

He smiled. "The last thing I want is to see my daughter's tears."

Leera took the coin. "I never know quite how you do that."

He winked. "Buy yourself something nice." He tried so hard not to show how sick he was. His words were strong, but his weak tone betrayed him.

"Like what? You've given me everything I could ever ask for." A truth she could not ignore. If anything, Hayden spoiled her. He could've easily resented the fact that he'd had a daughter instead of a son, but he hadn't. He loved her as if she were the best thing that ever happened to him.

"Not everything," Hayden said. "There are some things in this world, Leera, that only you can get for yourself."

Those words sunk into her chest, wormed into her heart. Not only could her father not give her all that she wanted, but he wouldn't be around to see her needs met and her happiness soar. Her eyes watered. Her bottom lip trembled ever so slightly.

"It's those damn tears again."

"They're persistent."

Hayden was dying, yet it was Leera who couldn't keep herself together. There would never be a braver man or a greater king than her father. Of that she had no doubt.

Queen Ursula came into the chamber. She sat on the opposite side of the bed. "Here," she said, offering a steaming cup to Hayden, "I brought you that tea you like."

"Thank you, my love." He sipped the tea and sighed in relief.

Ursula smoothed out the bedsheets. "You missed quite the tournament day. You should've seen Destrian."

"Oh, Mother." Did she have to bring that up now? Couldn't she see that her daughter was on the verge of tears?

"What? He was magnificent."

"He is a crowd favorite," Hayden said.

"The people love him," Ursula said. "He would make a fine king." She gave Leera a look as if she'd done something wrong. "You should pay more attention to him. Ask him to dance at your next party."

"I don't think we should have any more parties. It tires Father out."

Ursula gestured dismissively. "Nonsense. He's fine."

"No, he's not," Leera said, her tone firm.

Hayden cleared his throat. The tea helped clear out whatever clogged his lungs. "Maybe the king would like to speak for himself. And right now, the king is unsure."

"Have dinner with him, then," Ursula said to Leera, still harping on Destrian.

"No."

"Why not?"

"I don't want to." *He's not Alistair.*

"You should honour him. He's a valiant knight."

"If you like him so much then maybe you should marry him."

Ursula blinked. "Excuse me?"

Maybe Leera had gone too far, but she couldn't turn back now. How dare her mother barge in here and start spouting off about Destrian as the next king as if the current king—her husband, for Cosima's sake—were already dead?

"I don't want to talk about Destrian. He's not king. He hasn't won the tournament or my hand. And even if he did win the tournament, I wouldn't want to marry him anyway."

"Leera!" Ursula stood.

Leera jumped up too. "It's the truth. I don't care how great he'd be for king. He's nowhere near as great as my father!"

"Leera," Hayden said, "no one is replacing me."

But that was just it. That was the tournament's whole purpose. Replacement.

The tears came back again, and this time she had no hope of staving them off. Rather than subject her father to her sadness, she spun around and fled the chamber.

Steps sounded behind her out in the hall. Her mother chased after her. She grabbed Leera by the arm and forced her around.

"You'll marry whoever wins the tournament, and I don't give a damn if you love him or not," she said, glaring. "What do you think this is? You're a princess. Your duty is to your kingdom. Love? You don't know the first thing about it."

Leera wrenched her arm free. "And I suppose you do?" She laughed in her mother's face.

The fiery glare on Ursula's face extinguished, her expression clouding over. Leera felt a pang of guilt.

"I didn't love him when we first got married," Urusla said, softly. It sounded like a confession. "It was my duty as the daughter of a duke to marry him. But I do love him now. That's how love works, Leera. It grows. It doesn't start with a bang."

"But you married a great man," Leera said. "Destrian is nothing like Father."

"No, he isn't." Ursula's gaze dropped to the floor. "But you don't know everything about your father."

She said it as if there was a side to Hayden Leera didn't know. A side of him that had been kept secret, that would lessen him, tarnish him, make him into a man other than the father and king Leera adored and loved.

Leera wouldn't stand for it. "Don't you dare soil his reputation. My father is a hero!"

Ursula snapped her eyes up, piercing Leera like a lance to the heart. "Your father took me as a wife when I was already betrothed to his best friend and squire."

Leera's breath caught in her throat. Ursula meant Reynard, the knight that had trained Alistair, the knight that had been sent to Teerdock.

Leera shook her head. No, that couldn't be. Her father would never have taken a woman that had belonged to another. He never would have done something so dishonourable to his closest friend.

Yet when she searched Ursula's face for a crinkle of lie, she found nothing. Ursula told her the truth.

"That's who your father really is," Ursula said. "He took what he wanted because he had the greatness to do as he pleased. So you see, daughter, your father and Destrian aren't so dissimilar after all."

Chapter Twelve

"Reynard," Alistair said, his eyes on Leera seated at the royal terrace, "is it possible for someone to be more beautiful with each passing day?"

The queen accompanied her, but the king was not with them.

"Don't get your hopes up," Reynard said. "She is betrothed to someone and it may not be you."

Alistair was ready for a fight, and so were the other knights assembled in the list. Half the number of knights remained from the tournament's first day. The rest had either gone home or taken seats as spectators.

"I know it is me. He'd kissed her, he'd held her, and he knew her better than any other competitor.

Reynard turned to face him. He narrowed his gaze at him, as if searching for something in Alistair's expression.

Alistair blinked. "What?"

"Is there something you want to tell me?"

Alistair smiled. "Nothing at all." Like he'd ever tell Reynard what had happened in the castle's dungeons. That was a secret he'd take with him to the grave. He couldn't even imagine the rage Reynard would have for him if he knew the truth.

"Don't let your arrogance get the best of you."

"It's not arrogance. It's determination. Isn't that what you're always telling me to have? You ought to be proud of me."

Reynard tilted his head. "I would, if you'd tell me the truth."

"There's nothing to tell."

"Where do you go after the matches are won?"

"For a walk. Cool my head."

"A walk. Right. In a city you hate."

Alistair shrugged. "It's growing on me."

He looked back up at the royal terrace, but Leera was gone. Only two people represented the royal family: the Queen Ursula and the herald, who stepped up to the front and raised his hands in the air. The chatter silenced.

"The first match," the herald said, "will be against Sir Alistair Rudell."

Alistair stepped out, fist in the air. The crowds roared his name and he loved it. His chest warmed and his spirits soared. Who would be his victim today? Who would fall to his lance?

The crowd sobered and the herald announced Alistair's opponent.

"Against Sir Kythe Dermont."

If the crowd cheered for Kythe, Alistair did not hear them. Kythe broke through the grouped knights and turned to Alistair. He saluted him, with a wry smile gracing his lips.

"Friend against friend," Alistair said, still stunned.

"It's not how I would've wanted it," Kythe said.

"Good thing for me you don't want to win this tournament."

"True, but that doesn't mean I'll go easy on you."

The stable boys brought the horses out and Alistair mounted Snapper. Konrad passed him a lance and Alistair took it with a shaky hand. He gripped the lance hard, willing an end to the trembling. He had nothing to worry about. Kythe was just another knight. Just another opponent in his way to Leera. Kythe didn't even want to win. He had no interest in kingship or marrying Leera. He'd even *told* Alistair that.

Still, he said he wouldn't just let Alistair win either. And so what? Alistair could take him. Kythe wasn't even a big guy. In fact, he was the smallest of the knights. Tall, yes, but thin.

The herald slashed the flag and the first course began. Alistair dropped the visor down on his helmet and kicked Snapper into a gallop. They both charged down the list. Alistair cleared his mind, focused on the sound of the pounding earth and the spot on Kythe he wanted to strike.

He lowered his lance. Kythe did the same.

His lance hit—or so he thought.

He'd been hit himself. Right by the collar bone. The blow forced him to throw his head back. Cool wind slashed his face.

His helmet. Kythe had hit him so hard his helmet had come off. That had never happened to him before. His armor had protected him from any excruciating pain, but Kythe's aim had been perfect.

Knocking off an opponent's helmet counted for two points.

Damn it!

Alistair tossed his splintered lance. At least he'd managed to hit Kythe back. He turned his horse around to face Kythe.

Kythe lifted the visor on his helmet and smiled. "Like I said, I won't go easy on you. You'll have to earn your victory."

A squire picked up Alistair's helmet from the list and passed it to him, then gave him a fresh lance. The second course began and Alistair missed.

Thankfully, so did Kythe, but barely.

Alistair couldn't believe how good Kythe was, and he made it seem effortless. His movements were fluid, but calculated. He rode his horse with grace. He was like the knights depicted in ballads and poems. Like one of the Twelve Knights of Old. The knight Alistair had dreamed of becoming when he was a page.

The possibility that he might lose this match seemed high.

He had one trick that might work, a technique Konrad had taught him. It meant hitting low, and pushing the lance forward, carrying it through. The idea was to push the knight inwardly, so the knight would buck forward, lose his balance, and tip over. The trick was avoiding the shield, but that was with any technique. It also placed some strain on the knight using the technique, given that Alistair would have to lean into his strike, which might mean he'd lose his balance, too.

It was a risk, but one he was willing to take.

Resolved, he charged forward. In the moment before contact, he squeezed his knees tightly against Snapper then aimed low, leaning forward into his strike.

But Kythe moved his shield just in time, deflecting Alistair's attack.

The lance hadn't even splintered. The point hadn't made contact. It was just the blunt edge that had run along Kythe's shield.

That didn't count as a point.

Still two to one.

At least the move meant Kythe hadn't struck him, either.

Alistair lifted his visor and sucked air into his lungs. Sweat poured down the sides of his face. Jousting matches were not usually long, but even so, they were taxing on the body. Add desperation to the mix, and Alistair felt like he'd been running nonstop for an hour.

Konrad passed him his last lance for the last course. "You need to knock off his helmet or knock him off his horse."

"I know," Alistair said.

"Can you do it?"

"I don't have a choice, do I?"

"Make your next hit count."

Alistair nodded and snapped the visor shut.

The herald raised his flag and Alistair bent down to Snapper.

"We have to win. No matter what."

Snapper snorted.

The herald slashed the flag down.

For the fourth and final time, Alistair and Snapper tore down the list. Alistair gritted his teeth. He ignored his fear. Only one outcome would come out of this match. A world in which he lost could not exist. He believed that with all his heart.

He smashed the lance into Kythe's armor, felt Kythe's lance smash into him. He bucked back but Sybil's armor kept him safe. Alistair threw the splintered lance and twisted as far as he could to look behind him.

Kythe's horse trotted forward and Kythe had both his hands spread out. His shield slipped from his arm and he dropped his splintered lance. Then he tilted to the side and fell off his horse.

The crowd jumped from their seats and cheered Alistair's name. Konrad and Reynard, their faces beaming, ran toward Alistair.

He'd won.

But had he?

Kythe rolled over and got to his feet. He pulled off his helmet and patted the dirt and grass off his helmet. He lifted a gauntleted hand and nodded to Alistair.

No, Alistair hadn't won, not by his own skill. Kythe had let him win. He'd fallen off his horse on purpose. He could've fixed his balance in the saddle. He didn't have to fall. He chose to. He'd let Alistair win.

And he wanted Alistair to know it.

#

The tournament day was over and Leera made her way to meet Alistair in the dungeon as they had planned. She lumbered through the castle corridors, taking her time. It seemed colder than usual, despite the lit torches. She hugged her arms, listened to her footsteps echo off the walls.

The conversation with her mother was fresh in her mind. Her father would be replaced, and she had thought him impossible of faults. A perfect father, king, and husband. A man of greatness.

Yet, according to the queen, that wasn't entirely true.

"Hello, Princess."

She flinched at the word princess. She hadn't noticed Destrian leaning against the wall, arms crossed over his chest. Was he waiting for her? Had he been following her?

No. This corridor led to the wing of the castle set aside for the knights. They just happened to cross paths, or so she hoped.

"We missed you at the tournament today," Destrian said.

"I was taking care of Father," she lied. Her father had been sleeping during the tournament. She had been at the start of the tournament, but had left soon afterward, right before the first match was announced. She couldn't take it today. She couldn't watch men fight for the right to marry her. Before, she hadn't truly believed her father would use the tournament to marry her off, but after what Ursula had confessed, the idea didn't seem that farfetched.

"And how does the king fair?"

"Not well." She could've sworn the corner of his mouth curved upward. It was slight. Almost imperceptible. Maybe she imagined it.

She balled her hands into fists and carried on, passing Destrian.

"Where are you going?" he asked.

"Wherever I please," she said, in a biting tone.

"Princess, please, wait a moment."

Something in Destrian's plea stopped her. His voice sounded

softer, warmer. Not a tone she expected from Destrian's lips. He'd always seemed so frigid.

She turned to him. "Yes?"

"I know this must be a difficult time for you. I can't imagine what it must feel like to be in your position. It must feel like your whole world is falling apart."

It *was* falling apart. Her father was her world; he'd fought for, built, and given her a world to live in.

Destrian inched closer to her. "I'm sorry about your father. He is this kingdom. He built it with his own two hands. He is a great man." He took her hands in his, their silkiness caressing her. "None of the knights could even dream to be like him."

She looked up at him. He was taller than Alistair, a man of astute posture, proud to be of the nobility.

"But if I win this tournament, I will do everything I can to be the king he would want me to be. The king the Kingdom of Rowanark would need me to be. And the man you deserve to be with."

He ran the back of his hand over her cheek. It didn't feel off-putting at all, but quite tender. The same as when Alistair touched her.

Alistair—he waited for her now. She was late.

"I have to go," she said.

Destrian brought her hand to his lips. "Be safe and try not to worry so much. I promise you, this world that is falling apart, I will rebuild in the same likeness."

Promise me? she almost said, taken in by his words, words she wanted to believe could be true.

Maybe they could be.

She shook herself. She had to go and broke away from Destrian, leaving him in the corridor. She went to the dungeon, checking behind her, but no one followed her, no guards or soft-spoken knight.

A single candle barely lit the dungeon. Alistair sat by it, and he didn't look good. The candle's feeble light cast dark shadows across his face that lent him a dark, melancholy countenance.

That wasn't like her Alistair at all.

"What's wrong?" Had he lost his match today? "Did you…"

"I won," he said, his voice hoarse. He swallowed. "But barely."

He stood and went to her. He kissed her hard on the mouth, harder than ever before. His hands gripped her, rubbing roughly along her back and then her chest. He'd never touched her like that before. There was a need behind it. A need for validation.

He took her, claimed her, made her his, not caring what she thought or felt.

Was this how her mother felt when she'd made her sacrifice to the crown? When King Hayden, the hero of Rowanark, had claimed her as his wife, taking her from the man she'd been betrothed to, the man her father had called friend. Was this what duty felt like?

She shouldn't be doing this at all. She went behind her parents' backs to be with Alistair. She cheated the tournament, cheated her parents, cheated her own status and what was expected of her as a princess. This wasn't how a ruler of a kingdom conducted herself.

She put her hands on Alistair's chest and pushed him away.

"What's wrong?" he asked.

"I…I don't think I can do this anymore."

"Was it something I did?"

There was real concern behind those words. Concern for her. He sounded like the Alistair she remembered.

But it was too late. She'd gone down this path now and would see it to the end.

"I'm the Princess of Rowanark and yet I'm kissing a knight in secret." She smirked self-deprecatingly. "In a dungeon of all places."

"We could go elsewhere."

"You're missing the point."

"Then what is your point?"

There it was again—his desperation, his need. Not a need to be with her, but a need to feel worthy of himself.

"I'm a princess, and I have a duty to the crown."

"Since when do you care about duty?"

"I don't have to care about it. It's the life I was born into." All she had to do was accept it. An act harder than it sounded.

"A life you don't even like."

"What do you know what I like?"

"I know you like this." He ran a finger slowly over her jawline and a jolt ran through her. "And I know you like it when I kiss you here." He leaned in and took her earlobe in his mouth, sucking on it ever so slightly, but enough to make her breathe audibly. Yes, those were all things she liked. "I know things about you that no other person does. That you didn't know about yourself until we discovered it together."

How easy it would be just to fall into his arms, to give up her resolve and forget about everything? To go back to the first time they had snuck into the dungeon to be together?

But that time had passed. It should never have even been.

She slipped from his grasp and put distance between them. The closer she was to him, the weaker her resolve. "You're a knight, Alistair, and I'm a princess. You have your duties as a knight."

"Damn them," he said. "I have a duty to myself above all else, and that duty is telling me to be with you."

Duty to myself? She didn't have that luxury. She would be queen one day. One day soon. Her duty was to the people, to Rowanark. And if he intended to be king, then he, too, wouldn't have that luxury.

"You're so sure about winning this tournament," she said.

"I am."

"Even though you almost lost today."

He recoiled. Her tone hadn't been harsh, but the words had speared into him like hot knives.

"I need to know, Alistair. What makes you think you're worthy enough to replace my father?"

#

Worthy. The word echoed in Alistair's mind as he stepped away from Leera. Before the tournament, the knights and nobles saw him and his father as worthless. Some still did, like Destrian. The people of Rowan didn't even know where Teerdock was, or that it even existed.

Now they knew. It was why he'd come to this tournament, to prove his worth.

And then he'd met Leera again, and despite all else, she made him feel worthy. She made him feel like he had a place there, a place with the nobility, a right to the crown just like any of the others.

Except now—now she questioned his worth. Just like Kythe made him question his worth today. Just like he questioned his own worth every day, more and more.

Why was she acting this way? She'd never been this combative before.

"Has something happened to the king?" he asked. Leera was close to her father, and she loved him dearly. If the king's condition worsened, that would cause a rift in her heart.

"What do you care? What do *any* of you care? All you knights are after the same thing. His crown and to spread my legs."

Alistair cringed. "Is crude speech part of a princess's duty?"

She crossed her arms over her chest. "Don't tell me what I can and cannot say."

"What's gotten into you? This isn't like you."

"Oh, like you know me. I don't need you to fight for me, Alistair. I don't need you to win the tournament so I can be married to you, someone who will respect me enough to let me leave the castle on a leash."

"On a leash? You think that's why I compete?" He laughed. "I'm going to win the tournament because I love you."

She blinked. "Love me? You *love* me?"

"Yes." Of course, he loved her. She must have known that, yet he'd never said it to her before. Hearing the words out loud must have given her pause.

"And you'd stop at nothing for that love?" she asked.

"Nothing will get in my way." He owed it to Kythe.

Leera shook her head and looked up at the ceiling. "Why must all great men think that love must be conquered?"

What was she talking about? She said those words aloud but they seemed for her own ears, not for him to understand.

"What makes you great, Alistair?" she asked. "What makes you worthy?"

His throat clenched shut.

"You don't even know."

Alistair swallowed. "I fought a knight today," he rasped, "that I would call my friend, and even though I won, he was the better knight. He let me win, and he made sure I knew that."

Despite all his training and preparation, he was not yet worthy, not yet ready.

"Alistair…"

Pity colored Leera's voice, and it set his blood boiling.

"No, you're right," he said. "We shouldn't be doing this. I don't deserve your love. Not yet. I haven't earned it. I still need to prove myself." He glanced around the dungeon and chuckled to himself. "This is silly, isn't it? What am I doing in this dreary place kissing a princess? I should be training. Getting better. Becoming the man you can love. I don't just want to be a knight from some backwater fiefdom. Not anymore." He ran a hand through his hair. "I thought that was all I wanted, but you're right. I came here to prove I'm worthy to be a king, to take your father's place."

She glared at him. "You could never take his place."

"If I don't, Princess, someone else will."

He'd never called her Princess before. It was too formal, too proper. Too distant.

"I'm sorry, Princess. It's my fault you've strayed from your duties. For going behind the tournament's rules. It's not how a knight should act."

"No, it wasn't," Leera said, her gaze on the floor, her voice but a whisper. "It was how I wanted you to act."

Chapter Thirteen

That same night, the castle threw another party.

But calling this a party was an overstatement. The king, queen, and princess were missing. Few knights attended. The food sat on the tables growing cold and dry. No band played. It was quiet and eerie and reminded Alistair of a hermitage.

Alistair rolled his shoulders, then stretched his neck from side to side. After what happened with Leera, he had set up the quintain on the lists and ran at it with Snapper time and time again.

"You pushed yourself too hard today," Reynard said.

"I have to." But he'd have to rest a little tomorrow. Not just for himself, but for Snapper, too. "Yesterday, Kythe let me win."

"What?"

"He fell off his horse on purpose." Alistair tasted something bitter on his tongue. "He was the better knight."

"Why would he do that?"

Alistair shook his head. He didn't know, and Kythe had already left for Durham so he couldn't ask.

Would he have asked, though? Probably not. It took a lot out of him just to admit Kythe had given him the win.

Reynard patted Alistair's shoulder firmly. "No one said this would be easy."

"No." But Alistair had never witnessed a more graceful knight than Kythe. "He could've beaten me, Reynard."

And if he had, Alistair would've lost everything. He would've packed up his things and gone back to Teerdock, back to a life that no longer suited him, because Leera wasn't in it.

"Take it as a gift," Reynard said. "Now you have to win for his honour, too."

Alistair snorted. Too many people relied on his victory. Sybil and Walter. Konrad. Reynard. His father. Leera.

And now Kythe.

"I'm going to get something to drink." Alistair crossed the great hall toward one of the tables. As he did so, he passed Destrian, whose frigid stare unsettled him.

Just ignore him.

"You did well today, Alistair."

Alistair grimaced. So much for ignoring.

"Funny. I've never seen a knight fall so slowly off his horse. I must say, quite the delayed reaction."

Cold filled Alistair's veins. Destrian wore a smug grin on his face, his eyes alight with accusation. *He knows. The bastard knows.*

"Usually when a knight is knocked off his horse it's sudden. But not with Sir Kythe. It almost looked like he was debating whether to fall or not."

"I hit him," Alistair said, nearly growling.

Destrian tilted his head. "But did you hit him hard enough?"

Alistair lunged at Destrian, tackling him to the floor. Forget waiting for the tournament, he was going to beat Destrian here and now.

He vaguely heard Reynard calling out to him, demanding he stop.

But he didn't. He lifted his fist, ready to rain an inferno down on Destrian's pretty boy face—

And paused.

Leera stood by the arched doorway leading into the great hall. No one else saw her, just him. Everyone else had circled around him and Destrian.

The look on her face broke his heart. She was mortified, disgusted, and he was the cause.

She whirled around and fled.

Reynard grabbed Alistair by the collar of his tunic and hauled him off Destrian. The whole time Destrian laughed, even as he'd been about to get pummeled in the face.

"What do you think you're doing?" Reynard said, pulling him as far away from the rest as possible.

"He deserves it," Alistair said.

"On the list, yes, but not in the castle's great hall!"

Alistair pried himself free. "What's done is done." What a stupid thing to say. Reynard was right—he'd made himself look like a fool. He'd done exactly what Destrian wanted him to do. Did he feel better? On the contrary, he felt worse.

And Leera had looked at him like he was a monster.

He had to get out of there, had to find her and explain everything.

"Where do you think you're going?" Reynard asked.

"To my room." He hated lying to Reynard, but he had no choice.

Reynard grabbed him by the elbow. "Tell me what's going on with you." His tone softened, his eyes held apprehension. "I can help."

Alistair yanked his arm away. "Nothing is wrong with me. I'm fine. I just need to rest."

Without sparing a glance to Destrian or the other knights, Alistair went after Leera. Once he was out of sight of the great hall he picked up his pace and caught up with her.

"Leera, wait," he called. "Please, wait." He ran toward her. "Let me explain myself."

Leera spun around, a scowl marring her beauty. "Explain yourself? Is that how a knight acts?"

"It was wrong, I know. It was stupid and wrong and I shouldn't have done it."

"We shouldn't even be here." Leera cowered back, hugging herself and shooting looks around them. "If they see us together…"

"I'll leave," Alistair said, "but before I go I want you to know something."

She looked up at him. Good, she was willing to listen.

He took a breath. He'd screwed up enough today and now was the time to turn it all around.

"I can't replace your father. I don't think anyone can. I'm not sure what he did in his past, what sacrifices he had to make to create the Kingdom of Rowanark, but I know I could never do what he did. I don't have the same kind of greatness. I'm different, and because of that, I'm someone your father could never be."

She squinted at him. "And what's that?"

"The one person who loves you more than anything in this world."

"My father loves me."

Alistair nodded. "But not in the same way I do. I don't need to replace him on the throne or in your life. I need to be the king that keeps the peace, not creates it. I need to be the king who you can happily share your life with."

The tournament was never about him taking the throne from a dying king. It was about accepting all the work and sacrifice of a great king and building on it.

"And I don't know if I'm there yet. I don't know what my greatness is, how I'm worthy. But every time I look at you, every time I see you up on that terrace watching the tournament unfold, I know I'm in the right place, I know I'm where I'm supposed to be." He took her hands in his and held them to his chest. "I'm where you can see me, and I can see you, because when you're around I want to be better. A better knight and a better man and one day, Cosima willing, a better king."

"Alistair…"

What he'd said, he'd meant, his words infused with his truth and his love. Her gaze dropped to the floor. Emotions warred on her expression. Doubtless, she was stuck between how she should or shouldn't act.

"You don't have to say anything. I just wanted you to know that. I get it. You're a princess. You have duties that go beyond me, beyond us. At least for now. And that's fine. I'll be yours when this is all over. I can wait."

He squeezed her hands, then released her, turning away. He'd said what he'd wanted to say. Now all he had to do was win.

"I'm sorry, too."

Alistair blinked. "Sorry?"

A smile graced her lips, and it was a far better look than the one she'd given him at the great hall. "I was angry and I put it out on you. I don't want my father to die, and I hate that I can't change that. I have no control over it, just like everything else in my life."

She caught his hand in hers and brought it up to her cheek. She kissed his knuckles, calluses and all.

"I'm a princess with a broken heart whose father is dying. Being with you helped me forget that for a time. But I can't keep ignoring it. I can't pretend like these aren't his…his last days and that I won't be queen. That's my destiny. That's my duty. And if I had my choice for a king and a husband, it would be you."

Something in his chest soared at those words. All the aches and pains he had from his training no longer bothered him. In fact, he had energy enough to hit the quintain again.

"You have a choice," he said.

"I don't."

"You can choose to believe I'll win. You can choose to put your faith in me."

She stepped closer to him. "I already have."

He wrapped his arms around her and held her. "Then I promise I'll make that the best choice you've ever made, a choice no one can ever take away from you."

"We can't be seen together," she said.

"I know. Do you want to go to—"

"Yes."

He pulled back from her, surprised she agreed. "I'll go first and meet you there?"

"Give me twenty minutes. Bring a candle?"

"Done." Swiftly, Alistair went back to his room, lit a candle, and made his way to the dungeons. As he reached the stairs he thought he heard something. Footsteps. He checked his surroundings, thought he saw a shadow recede. He doubled back. Nothing.

Was it Leera? No. She wouldn't hide. What about a patrolling guard? He'd never seen one before. Probably just the shadows cast from the candle.

He descended the stairs and waited for Leera.

Not long after, she arrived.

Without a word, he went to her, touched her gently, and kissed her. With her hands, she explored his back, and it felt nice on his muscles to have her hands run across his aches. He kissed her again and again. He wouldn't stop. He didn't want to. He'd gone through a day in the Great Depths, and he would've done it all over again if it led to this moment.

In this moment of complete bliss.

"Alistair!"

Alistair jerked, and both he and Leera broke free of each other.

Reynard stood by the staircase, his face a mask of fury.

#

Leera gasped. Her chest rose and fell with labored breathing. She tugged her hair behind her ears, smoothed out her dress, tried to make herself as presentable as possible.

Too late. They'd been caught. Someone had seen them come down to the dungeon and followed them.

"Reynard?" Alistair said.

Leera's stomach dropped. This man standing before them was Reynard. The man who was knight-mentor to Alistair. The man who had squired with her father. The man who had been betrothed to her mother.

She never knew him, and now he stood before her with barely contained rage.

"How could you do this?" he said in a scorching tone that made Leera quiver. "Do you have any idea what would've happened if you were caught by one of the king's guard? Or by one of the other knights? King Hayden would hang you!"

"I—"

Reynard didn't let him finish. "You disgrace your father with this action. And you disgrace me as your knight-tutor. How long has this been going on? How long, Alistair?" He slammed a fist against the stone wall. "Answer me!"

Alistair stood straight, lifting his jaw. "Long enough to mean something."

Reynard smirked. "To mean something? You have a real chance of winning the tournament, of becoming king, and then you go and do something like this?" He shook his head. "This is not how a King of Rowanark should act. This isn't how a knight should act. I thought you were changing, becoming a better man, understanding what it truly meant to be a knight… I should've known better."

"I'll still win the tournament."

"Becoming king means more than just winning a tournament and marrying the princess."

Leera opened her mouth to defend Alistair. She was as much to blame for their actions. But Alistair spoke up first.

"Nothing we've done is wrong. We love each other."

"Love? You haven't earned the princess's love. If I could, I would strip your title as a knight right here and now. Nothing about this is fit for a knight or a king."

"Says the legendary Sir Reynard who slept with the king's wife."

Reynard bristled. That Reynard's anger could reach a new height seemed impossible, but it did. He looked ready to strangle Alistair with his bare hands.

But Alistair didn't know everything of what happened between Reynard and her mother. Neither did Leera, but she knew Reynard had been wronged, rather than the wrong-doer.

"You're a fool," Reynard said. "A reckless, arrogant, childish fool. My past is the reason I'm here now. The reason I followed you. I knew something was going on. I wanted to protect you, Alistair. I wanted to make sure you didn't make the same mistake I did."

"How could love be a mistake?"

Reynard grabbed Alistair by the collar of his tunic. "Forget about love, Alistair. This will never happen again." He shoved Alistair aside then bowed his head to Leera. "My apologies, Princess."

"It wasn't his fault." Her voice shook.

"Maybe," Reynard said, "but it is not my place to punish you. And if you do truly love each other, then you won't do this ever again."

Chapter Fourteen

"Ready for the finals?"

If Alistair could scream "For the love of Cosima, no" to the knight who asked him that question, he would have. Instead, he kept his mouth shut. Some knights who had stayed to watch the rest of the tournament were gathered outside the knights' residence. A few castle guards stood around, too, talking among themselves until Alistair stepped outside and they came closer. He was becoming a man of renown.

Tomorrow was the tournament's last day, and he was up against none other than Destrian.

He'd defeated every single knight he came across. They'd all fallen to his lance, one at a time.

Just one more left. Then he could be with Leera. He hadn't seen her since Reynard had caught them.

"Come tomorrow we might be calling you, 'Your Majesty,'" a guard said.

Alistair shrugged. "We'll see. Hopefully, I'd make a good king."

"We think so," a knight said.

"You do?" A compliment from the nobility? He wasn't used to it, but he could grow accustomed.

"Look," another knight said, "we know we've always given you a hard time, Alistair."

Name calling, bullying, making him feel less than human. That was more than just giving him a hard time.

"But it was undeserved," the knight continued. "If I could take it back, I would."

Alistair sensed no guile. "You all feel this way?"

The knights nodded. Some of them couldn't even look Alistair in the eyes, those who had been among the meanest, members of Destrian's entourage who were no longer with him.

"It's not just because you might become king. We've gotten to know you better. You're a good man, Alistair."

A good man? But what about a great man?

Tomorrow he would know, but today he had to train with Konrad.

"Thank you," he said. "That means a lot to me." Years of bullying slowly melted away from him. He let it go, glad to do so.

"Don't go all misty eyes on us now," a knight said. "A king doesn't cry."

Alistair smirked. "I'll remember that."

They already thought of him as their next king. They believed in him. He could count them as friends and fellow knights.

Alistair was about to excuse himself when he heard a commotion at the front gate.

"You're not allowed in the castle, traitor," the guard said.

Traitor?

A handful of guards blocked the front gate from letting Sybil in. She looked beyond the guards and her eyes locked onto Alistair's. She pushed through, but the guards held her back.

"Alistair! Hey!" She waved to him, smiling, and then scowled when a guard put his hands on her. "Would you let go of me? I'm with the man who could very well be your future king. Alistair!"

One of the guards from the gates came up to Alistair, a sheepish look on his face. "I'm sorry, Sir Alistair, but it appears she is here for you."

"Why do you call her a traitor?"

"She is the brother of the traitor Reynard. King Hayden has banished her from the castle."

"But Reynard is with me at this tournament."

"True, but he is also your knight-tutor, and so the king has allowed it. Our orders have not changed when it comes to his sister."

"Alistair!" Sybil cried out. "Tell them I'm with you! I have a new type of armor for you!"

So that was why she was there. But his armor was fine. It got him this far and with little to no pain. He had one day left in the tournament, why would he need new armor? She shouldn't have come. It was too risky.

"Should we let her through?" the guard asked.

If they did, news of it might reach the king that Alistair had allowed her through. No use in putting more grief on King Hayden. Especially now, while Alistair was in everyone's good graces.

"No," Alistair said. "If the king doesn't wish for her to be in the castle, then she shouldn't be here."

The guard nodded. "A wise decision, Sir Alistair."

If it was so wise, why did it leave a sick feeling in his gut? The nobles treated him like an equal. He couldn't ruin it now by letting in someone branded a traitor by the king. Still, didn't this make *him* into a traitor? Wasn't he now betraying Sybil? She'd done so much for him.

He ought to go outside Castle Rowanark and speak with her.

"Alistair, come on!" Konrad called from the inner ward. He waved him over. "You've got training to do."

He had one last day to train and brush up on his skills. The armor he had now from Sybil had gotten him all the way to the finals. What would be the point in changing now? He'd need to go with Sybil to her house, go through a fitting on the new armor, and then come back to the castle to train. It was too much time wasted. He was used to his armor now. It had brought him outstanding luck. He didn't want to part with it.

"I'm sorry," he whispered so none of the other knights would hear him.

He would fix this. Once he became king, Sybil could stay at the castle if she wanted. Be his personal armorer.

But for now, he had to turn his back on her.

#

The lance splintered off Alistair's shield, the impact so fierce it knocked him off Snapper. He hit the ground hard, lying flat on his back.

Instead of jumping back up, he laid there, spread-eagled, looking up at the cloudy skies.

Was Rowan always cloudy? So unlike Teerdock, which was sunny most days of the year. He closed his eyes. Did he really want to stay in a city that rained all the time? It would probably pour tomorrow for the last day of the tournament.

On his horse, Konrad trotted over to Alistair and peered down at him. "What in the Great Depths is wrong with you?"

What in the Great Depths *was* wrong with Alistair? He'd been training for the past hour with Konrad and he hadn't won a single course. This wasn't like him.

"If this is how you plan on fighting tomorrow, you might as well give the crown over to Destrian."

Alistair rolled over and got to his feet, then picked up his shield. He'd gotten so far. Farther than anyone thought he would get, even himself. He had fans and people who counted on him to win. He couldn't just lie down and let Destrian take from him everything he had tasted and now wanted to keep.

Speaking of Destrian, he stood out in the ward with Brom, watching Alistair train. Alistair shot him a glare. Didn't he have anything better to do? File his nails? Oil and comb his hair? Get fitted for a pair of silk trousers? Anywhere but there. And why wasn't he training?

At least he didn't have any lackeys with him. Only Brom. The rest of the knights stayed mostly neutral to either Alistair or Destrian.

"Let's do it again," Alistair said.

"You're damn right we're doing it again."

Alistair gripped Snapper's reins, but the horse pulled away, yanking Alistair's arm. "Ow. Stupid horse!"

The cruel words came out of his mouth faster than he could take them back. As if he could understand, Snapper bared his teeth at Alistair.

Alistair sighed. "I'm sorry. I didn't mean that." With hands up in the air, he approached Snapper carefully. Knowing Snapper, he was liable to kick Alistair in the chin. Not like Alistair didn't deserve it. "I just, you know, haven't seen her in a while."

Leera hadn't come to any of the tournament matches, and neither had the king. Snapper snorted, and Alistair ran his hand along Snapper's smooth mane. "One more day, and then you'll never have to be ridden by me again."

Snapper moved back a step so Alistair could climb up the stirrups and mount.

Alistair took his place at the end of the list. A page passed him a lance. He and Konrad ran the course.

But he missed, and Konrad's lance smashed into him.

At least this time he didn't fall off.

"Unbelievable," Konrad said. "It's like you've forgotten everything I've taught you."

"There's a lot on my mind, all right?"

"I'm sure there's only one thing on your mind," Reynard said, his arms crossed over his chest, "and she has a name."

He meant Leera.

"You'd better clear your head quick or you may lose it to your opponent." Konrad tossed his chin to Destrian. "Let's try this again. This time aim for my collar bone."

Alistair stiffened. That was the same move Kythe had used on him, the one that knocked his helmet off. Couldn't he try a different move?

They ran the course another time. Alistair hesitated with his aim and hit Konrad's shield and got hit himself.

Konrad shook his head. "You're a disappointment."

"I'd say," Reynard said. "And he calls himself a knight."

"I am a knight," Alistair said between gritted teeth.

"Who can't ride a horse or carry a lance or live a truthful and honourable life."

"Forget this." Alistair tossed his broken lance. He swung off Snapper. "I don't need to train, I need to rest. Unless there's anything new you want to teach me here?"

"I've taught you everything I know," Konrad said.

"Good. Then we're done here." After all, if Destrian didn't need to train for Alistair, Alistair didn't need to train for Destrian.

"All knights need to train," Konrad said.

Alistair pointed to Reynard. "Well, according to my esteemed knight-tutor, my knight ceremony was a sham, and I'm not a real knight."

"He was kidding. Weren't you, Reynard?"

Reynard was silent, his jaw set. That was all he did these days, glare and scowl and shake his head in disappointment. How Reynard viewed him shouldn't bother him. Who cared if he disappointed

Reynard? Who was Reynard to him? He never gave a damn about Alistair when he was a squire, and he sure didn't give a damn about him now. Reynard had made that abundantly clear.

"Okay," Konrad said, "maybe he does mean it. More reason for you get back on your horse."

"I'm done for the day."

Konrad's nostrils flared. "Get back on your horse, boy."

Alistair slashed the air with his arm. "I've done enough training! I've gotten this far, haven't I? No one thought I would, but I have. I don't need you to help me anymore. I don't need any of you. I will win on my own."

Damn it, he felt like he'd just fallen face first into a pile of horse manure. First with Sybil this morning and now with Reynard and Konrad. Reynard had started it, though. If only his knight-tutor would get over his relationship with Leera. Alistair hadn't seen her once since then. Not once. And did he ever need to see her.

Instead of seeing Leera, he'd go for a walk. Do something to clear his head. As he passed Destrian and Brom he couldn't help but glance over at them.

Destrian smiled coldly, while Brom's eyes had a dark glint in them.

It gave Alistair the shivers.

#

"My kids love you," said the man drinking at the bar seated next to Alistair. "You're their favorite knight."

Alistair lifted his mug and flashed a smile. "Thanks. That means a lot to me."

The tavern reminded him of Wendel's back at Teerdock. He missed that about home. Not the drinking or the tavern, but the people. Getting drunk and swapping stories let him forget for a time that he wasn't the best of knights. He was one of them. In other words, they liked and respected him.

He came for the mead but stayed for the validation.

Did great men need validation? Probably not. As for him, he lived off it.

"Isn't tomorrow the finals?" the man asked.

"Indeed, it is," Alistair said.

The man's forehead puckered as he watched Alistair down his drink. "Should you be drinking the night before the big day?"

"This is only my second drink." A lie. He'd had a few more than that. He should stop, though. His head swam but didn't drown, and his muscles warmed and loosened. It was a good spot to be in. Any further and he might find himself slurring with one eye open, telling everyone in the tavern how much he loved them loving him.

"Have you ever taken your family to Teerdock?" Alistair asked the man.

"Where?"

"Teerdock. Where I'm from. The fiefdom I represent."

"Oh, no, no. We pretty much stay close to the fiefdoms around Rowan."

Not surprising. Did the maps in Rowan not go as far as Teerdock? Only one person knew about Teerdock—the King.

"Can I get you another?"

"No, no." Alistair burped into his fist. "I think that's enough for me."

"Good luck tomorrow."

"I trust you'll be there?"

"Yes, me and the family, my lord."

Alistair smiled, patted the man's back. "Hope to see you."

He paid his tab and wove through the tables to the exit. The cool night woke his senses, sobering him. Wrapping his cloak around him, he made his way back to the castle gates.

The street leading to the castle was the main market street and while it bustled with activity in the morning and afternoons, it was jarringly quiet at night. Such a transformation of two extremes. The store fronts were closed, and while there were residences above, people were either sleeping or out to the taverns.

Alistair's stomach churned. He shouldn't have had that last mead. But he didn't want to go back to his room at the castle, either. He'd never seen Reynard this angry at him before. Angry, and disappointed, and more so than usual. Reynard was always a bit disappointed in Alistair, like Alistair wasted his talent helping the farmers in Teerdock when he ought to be out questing like a real knight. But this time, the disappointment was like that of a father to a son who had disobeyed and disgraced him. No doubt, if Reynard told his father about Leera, that was exactly what would happen with his real father.

Booted steps and a black cloaked figure emerged from the alleyway in front of Alistair. A scarf covered the man's face, except for his eyes, which stared Alistair down. He towered over Alistair and was nearly twice his size in muscle.

Alistair's chest sank. Great. Before dealing with Reynard's ire, he had to contend with a common mugger.

No. He had waited for Alistair. He wanted Alistair.

"Do you know who I am?" Alistair said.

"I do. That's why I'm here."

The voice was muffled, but it sounded familiar.

Alistair narrowed his eyes. Maybe not a common mugger after all.

The cloaked figure drew a sword from his belt, moonlight glinting off the blade. Alistair stepped back. This wasn't good. The figure's intent was clear. Alistair reached for his own sword—

And grasped air. He'd been in such a hurry after his training with Konrad, that he'd left his sword in his room. He had nothing to defend himself with. Not even a knife. Just his bare hands.

The cloaked figure charged at him, swinging his sword. Alistair jumped back, but the attacker pressed on. Alistair avoided each slash, but only barely, his movements sloppy from the mead. He had to get out of there and back to the castle.

But he couldn't get around the attacker. It was one thing to block sword attacks with a shield or parry them with a sword, but an entirely different matter when unarmed and garbed in only a tunic.

The cloaked figure lunged, his sword snaking out. Alistair tried to dodge the attack but he was too slow. The blade cut a deep gash into his side.

He cried out, gripping the cut. He pulled his hand away and blood covered his fingers and palm. A burning pain filled his stomach. The wound left him unsteady.

The cloaked figure kicked out with his boot. Alistair fell onto his back. He struggled to get up, but the figure slammed a foot down on Alistair's chest, putting all his heavy weight on that one foot.

Alistair coughed, then gasped for air. The strain on his lungs was crushing.

With both hands, the cloaked figure raised his sword in the air. There was no mistaking the look in the man's eyes.

Murder.

Chapter Fifteen

The attacker's sword spiraled downward in a silver arc. Closing his eyes, Alistair waited for the blade.

If only he'd had one last chance to tell Leera how much he loved her, how much she meant to him, and how thankful he was that she had been in his life.

"Ah!"

His attacker screamed in pain. A sword clattered on the cobblestones.

Alistair snapped his eyes open. The attacker gripped the wrist of his right hand, a throwing knife jabbed into his hand. Blood splattered on the cobblestones.

A split second later, Konrad slammed into the attacker with his shoulder, pushing him off Alistair.

"Get up, Alistair!" Reynard called, a sword drawn.

Konrad hauled Alistair up, and sharp pain shot through him. He hissed.

"Are you hurt?" Konrad said.

Alistair gripped his side. His head swam. Exhaustion gripped him. His legs shook and his knees buckled, lurching him forward.

Konrad put an arm around him and caught him. His eyes widened. "He's bleeding!" He pointed at the attacker. "I'm going to kill you."

Even though, unlike Reynard, Konrad was unarmed and held Alistair in his arms, his threat sent chills down Alistair's spine. The cold way he had said it made it seem more like a promise than just a threat.

The attacker stood up and the scarf around his face loosened, revealing more of the attacker's identity.

It was dark, and Alistair's vision blurred, but he could've sworn he saw Brom.

His stamina giving out, Alistair collapsed into Konrad's arms, weighing Konrad down.

The attacker's escaping foot falls echoed off the cobblestone street as darkness engulfed Alistair.

#

Alistair awoke in a daze. The ceiling above him floated down as if to crush him and then buoyed back up. He blinked to clear his vision, then glanced around him.

Where was he? Back in his room at the castle. How did he get there? Only Cosima knew. Had he really been that drunk last night?

Reynard sat in a chair by the bed, one leg crossed over the other. Dark circles clouded his eyes.

Alistair put his hands under him and lifted himself up, but only got a few inches off the mattress before pain seared through his ribs. He collapsed.

"What happened?" he asked, licking his dry lips. He rubbed at where the pain radiated. Bandages were wrapped around him.

"A mugging," Reynard said.

Alistair remembered now. He'd had a few drinks but not enough to get him drunk, and then on his way to the castle, he'd been attacked by…

Brom? Had that been the identity of the attacker? Alistair had caught a glimpse before passing out. Did Konrad and Reynard catch him?

"That was no mugging," Alistair said.

"I agree. Someone wants you dead."

Dead? Or…

Sunlight beamed into the room. Instead of morning birdsong, there was chatter, laughter, and yelling. It was the next day, the tournament's last day. And what was Alistair doing? Lying in bed.

Today was his day to prove himself to the kingdom. With fists to either side of him he pushed himself up, groaning. The pain blazed through him. He had to get up and stretch it out.

"What did I tell you?" Reynard said. "Stay down and rest."

"I can't. I have a tournament to win."

"You're in no position to compete."

"You expect me to forfeit?" He'd rather die.

"No. We'll request a postponement. Clearly you can't be expected to fight in your condition."

That was exactly what Destrian wanted. Not a mugging, indeed. He didn't have any proof, but he could swear on his life the attack last night was connected in some way to Destrian.

"Do we know who did this?" Alistair asked.

"I can guess."

"So can I." Alistair got to his feet and pitched forward.

Reynard caught him. "What did I tell you?"

Alistair gripped Reynard's arms, helping him to stand. "We need to ask the king for a postponement, don't we? He'll want to see me."

"Alistair, you should stay in bed. I will speak to the king."

"Ha, are you joking? Neither you nor Konrad could speak to the king without being thrown in prison. I have to do it."

Reynard took a moment to consider and then nodded his head. He helped Alistair dress in a tunic and trousers, then swung Alistair's arm around his shoulder and they left.

Climbing down the stairs was torturous, every step like a stabbing from a hot knife. But as they got to the bottom, the pain lessened. Once outside, Alistair stepped away from Reynard and stretched.

"Damn, it hurts."

"The wound isn't deep, so it'll heal quickly. But if you irritate it, you'll only make things worse for yourself."

"Let's just get this postponed."

They entered the list, the terraces crammed with spectators. On the first day, the list had been teeming with knights and their entourage. Now it was only Alistair, Reynard, Konrad, Destrian, and his squire. The crowds quieted as Alistair entered.

As they approached the royal stand, Konrad gave Alistair a worried look. Alistair nodded assurance to him.

Queen Ursula stood from her seat, the herald by her side. Leera sat at the edge of her seat, as beautiful as ever. King Hayden was missing. Even on the last day of the tournament, he was too sick to attend.

"Where's King Hayden?" Alistair asked Reynard.

"We'll make our request to the queen."

"In that case, maybe you should do the talking."

Reynard grunted a chuckle. That was a first for him. "Don't make me finish what the mugger started."

"It is true, then," the queen said, her voice booming out to the list. "You were attacked last night."

"Yes, my lady," Alistair said.

Destrian snorted. "Sure you didn't trip while you were drunk?"

Alistair shot him a dark look.

"And where's your brother, Sir Destrian?" Reynard asked. "I find it hard to believe your own flesh and blood would miss your last day at glory."

That shut the bastard up. He glared at Reynard but kept his lips mashed together.

"What would you have me do, Sir Alistair?" said the queen.

Alistair opened his mouth but the words were stuck in his throat. He couldn't ask for a postponement. It was weak. Everyone came here today to see him. What kind of future king would disappoint the people? What kind of knight would turn his back on a fight?

The queen watched him expectedly.

"My Queen," said Reynard, and Ursula looked at him with wide eyes, the color draining from her face, "I would request a postponement of today's match."

The crowd groaned and booed. The people of Rowanark wanted a fight. How dare the nobility try and take it away from them?

Ursula raised her hands, quieting the crowd. "Postponement?" Her voice was tight, her hands were trembling. It must've been years since she'd spoken to Reynard. She was visibly stricken.

"Just until Sir Alistair is recovered," Reynard said. "It will not take long, I promise you."

"My Lady," Destrian piped up, "I was told this morning by the surgeon that the wound Alistair suffered was nothing more than a flesh wound. Knights are inflicted with such wounds all the time and continue their duties without delay. To grant a postponement now, particularly while the king's condition has grown worse, is unnecessary and only delays the inevitable."

"Which is?" Alistair asked, finding his tongue.

Destrian flashed him a wolfish smile. "My victory."

Bastard.

"My Queen," Reynard said, "I'm not sure which surgeon Sir Destrian spoke to, but I assure you, Sir Alistair is in no position to compete this day."

"I would hear it from Sir Alistair," Ursula said, tearing her gaze from Reynard. "Knowing that the king's condition worsens, would you delay the people of Rowanark their future king? Will you fight this day?"

Alistair looked at Destrian, who wanted him to say yes, wanted him to fight in his current weaken condition. Then he glanced at Leera. The real question was, could he delay another day without Leera?

She shook her head. A slight movement, barely perceptible, but he caught it. She wanted him to yield this day.

"Say no," Reynard whispered to him.

But he couldn't. This was the moment he'd fought so hard for. He wouldn't disappoint the people, his fans. The people who loved him.

"I will fight, my lady," he said.

Ursula smiled, nodding. "Very well. Good luck, and may the best jouster win."

Leera blanched, and it pained him to see it. But the crowd—their cheers boosted his strength, helped him to forget his injury.

"Have you lost your mind?" Reynard said.

"I'll be fine," Alistair said.

"You'll get yourself killed."

"Sybil's armor will protect me."

"Alistair, please. Don't do this."

Alistair shook his head. The pages and squires ran around preparing the list. A stable boy brought out Snapper. "There's no turning back now."

"This is exactly what Destrian wants to happen. Don't you see? He orchestrated this whole thing. Brom was the one who attacked you."

"You think I don't know that? What would you have me do? You heard the queen. King Hayden doesn't have much time, and

Rowanark needs a new king. Don't worry. I won't let Destrian win."

"I worry, Alistair. I've always worried about you."

"Then stop. Now, will you help me put my armor on or not?"

Chapter Sixteen

Alistair mounted Snapper and winced as the pain in his side throbbed. He cursed under his breath. In all his visions of how this day would unfold, this was not one of them. He'd just gotten on the horse and already he sweated and breathed laboriously.

"You don't have to do this, Alistair," Reynard said.

He did. The people of Rowanark expected him to compete. He glanced over at Leera and she watched him with wide, frightened eyes. In a weird way, it was nice to know she worried about him. "He's given me no choice," he said, as a page passed him his full helmet.

"And if you lose?"

"I won't." But he could hear the shred of doubt in his own voice. He cleared his throat.

Konrad came up to him, his expression full of dismay as he petted Snapper.

"Please tell me you have some secret move you want to impart," Alistair said.

"I've taught you everything I know. You are a strong fighter, Alistair. You would've made a fine soldier in the Black Knight's army."

Alistair cocked his head to the side. "I'll take that as a compliment."

Konrad put a hand over Alistair's gauntleted one. "Aim true and strike hard."

Alistair nodded. "I will."

"Good luck."

Alistair put on his helmet and dropped the visor. On the opposite side of the list, Destrian, garbed in silver plated armor, his helmet sprouting horns, sat on his black charger and grinned at Alistair.

Smile all you like, you bastard. It won't last long.

Konrad passed him his lance. Tension seized his body, which only worsened the pain in his wound. Biting his lip, he tried to ignore it. Jousting matches did not usually take a long time to finish. He could suffer through this and push past the pain.

The herald lifted his flag. Everything was quiet, suspended in anticipation. Today, history would be made.

The flag slashed down and Alistair kicked Snapper into a gallop. He stormed down the list, lowered his lance, and aimed for Destrian.

He felt his lance make contact and at the same time, a great force crashed into him, pushing him back. He managed to stay on his horse, but the blow had felt unlike any of the other times he'd been hit.

It hurt tremendously.

#

Leera felt the terrible blow as if Destrian had struck her with his lance himself. She gripped the arms of the chair and ground her teeth. Her pulse raced and blood pounded in her ears so loudly it drowned out the crowd's cries, roars, and cheers.

Alistair rotated his shoulder, hunched over while mounted on Snapper. He looked…bad. He lacked the sturdiness he'd had before. He'd been like an impenetrable wall. But now that wall began to crack.

What was he thinking, taking on this fight? Was he doing this for her? What if he lost? At this rate, he would lose. He couldn't do it in the condition he was in.

She shook her head. No, she wouldn't think like that. She had to be brave for him. Be the strength for him that he lacked so that when he looked up at her he could find the courage to push onward because she believed in him.

If only she could go down to the list and be there with him.

Alistair…

"Princess."

A guard startled her and she whirled around to him. What could be more important right now than this match?

But the grave look on the guard's face filled her veins with ice.

The king. Something was wrong with her father.

"Is everything all right with my father?" she asked.

"He calls for you, Princess. He bids you to attend to him."

"What's happened?" She so badly wanted to hear something hopeful, no matter how much of an impossibility that was.

"Princess, he does not look well." The guard licked his lips. He was scared or anxious. "Please hurry."

Her throat clenched shut, cutting air to her lungs. Hurry? That could only mean one thing.

She looked down at Alistair as a squire passed him his lance. She wanted to stay and watch him compete. He needed her.

But her father needed her, too, and though the guard hadn't said it, she knew this may be her last chance to be with him.

Please hurry. She shot up from her chair, and it took every fibre of her being to turn away from Alistair.

But that was exactly what she had to do, and she did not look back.

#

The pain radiated from Alistair's ribs and spread across his chest and stomach. He sucked in air, his chest heaving, and with each heave a stab of pain.

He'd managed to break his lance off Destrian, but unlike him, Destrian sat poised on his horse, unhurt, already reaching for a fresh lance.

The herald raised his flag, indicating the start of the second course. Queen Ursula was there, too, sitting at the edge of her seat as if she was about to jump up at any moment. And Leera—

She was gone. She'd been there at the start, he was sure of it. Had she left? Why? Why would she leave him? This was the most important moment of not only Rowanark, but of her life.

His ribs flared up and he hissed. It hurt more than it should have. Not just his injury, but his chest, too. His armor had protected him before, so why wasn't it doing its job now?

He shook his head. He couldn't think on that now. A squire offered him a lance. He reached for it with a trembling hand. Retracting his hand, he clenched it into a fist, willing the shaking to stop. He took two slow, quivering breaths, then took the lance.

The flag dropped and the second course began. Destrian bolted down the list. Alistair kicked Snapper and together they charged.

As he closed in on Destrian, Alistair lowered the lance as he had done dozens of times before but this was different. The pain burned into him, numbing his arm. His grip weakened and the point of the lance dropped. He could barely lift it up.

He had to drop the lance, but it was too late. They came at each other too fast.

His lance veered, missing Destrian entirely.

And Destrian's lance slammed into him with full force.

\#

The sight of her father frightened Leera. Frightened her because she knew what was coming and wasn't prepared for it.

King Hayden lay in his bed, wheezing. Dark circles ringed his eyes, and his cheeks were hollow. He'd lost a lot of weight in such a short time. He was only a sliver of the father Leera knew and cherished. A shadow of the Wizard King that protected Rowanark and its people.

The guard left them alone. Gently, Leera lowered herself down on the bed next to him. Suddenly everything that was going on— with the tournament, with her and Alistair, with her and Destrian, with her and her mother—none of it mattered. It all seemed trivial.

Hayden opened his eyes slowly. He licked his dry, cracked lips and swallowed. He reached for her. "Daughter…"

Leera tenderly took his hand in both of hers. "Daddy."

She hadn't called him that in years. Not since she'd been a child. How she wished she could go back to those days now, when she thought her father was the strongest, healthiest man alive.

The guard was right. There wasn't much time left.

"I should get Mother," she said.

"No. I don't want you to leave."

A desperate plea, and it made her heart crack.

She nodded. "I'm going to stay right here."

"Do you want to see a magic trick?"

She smiled. Even now her father tried to cheer her up when it should've been the other way around. "Do you want to see me in disguise?"

"I do. I want to see you become the queen I know you can be."

Yet he wouldn't. He would never see her grow into a woman. A wife. A mother. A queen. He would never see his grandchildren. The sickness robbed so much from him. But it wouldn't rob this moment from him, the last moments between father and daughter.

"I will be," she said. "I've only ever wanted to do right by my father. Cosima knows I gave you more grief than any daughter should."

He chuckled meekly. "You were always a good girl."

"I wasn't and you know it. I rebelled. I made your life miserable. And through it all, you never raised your voice once to me. You were never angry with me. You never made me feel afraid of you." Tears welled up in her eyes. Emotion thickened her tone. "I love you, daddy. I love you so much."

"I love you, too, sweetheart. Never forget that." His voice hardened, as if he were fighting off his sickness to make his words sound strong and true and everlasting. "Never think I wanted a son instead of you. I'm happy I had you in my life and only you. You made all my sacrifices worth it, and if I had a chance, I would do it all over again and change nothing."

She cried. She cried so much she didn't think she would ever stop. The tears blurred her vision, marred the image of her father, and she didn't want to miss a second of him. She wiped and wiped but still the tears shed.

Her father lifted his delicate hand to her cheek and brushed the tears away and like magic they stopped and she could see her father clearly, a vague smile on his face.

"I'm so proud of you." He rubbed her cheek with his thumb. "Rowanark is in good hands."

She held his hand in both of hers. She kissed his knuckles, clung to him.

Keep holding on, daddy. Keep holding on.

Slowly the grip faded and his eyelids lowered. He looked like he was sleeping. A peaceful, dreamless sleep.

#

After the second round, Alistair, with Snapper, trotted back to the end of the list rubbing his breastplate.

"By Cosima, that was brutal," he said.

Konrad's eyes widened. "You're bleeding."

Bleeding? He looked down and sure enough blood stained the armor plates on his thighs. His wound must've reopened.

"That's it." Reynard threw his hands in the air. "This match is over. I'm calling it off."

"No!" Alistair said. "If you do that, Destrian wins."

"He's already winning and you're bleeding."

"He hasn't beaten me yet." Alistair extended his hand out. "Lance!"

"If you die, your father will kill me," Reynard said.

"If I don't do this now, how can I go on living?"

Reynard scoffed. "Don't be so damn melodramatic."

Alistair shrugged. "You started it."

"Insufferable brat!"

Konrad gently pushed Reynard aside and passed Alistair a fresh lance. "Don't try anything risky. Hit him on the side and try to spin him off his horse. Right here." He pointed to the target area. "Between shoulder and breast."

Alistair nodded, taking the lance. "Thanks."

He sat up straight on the saddle and tested the weight of the lance with his injury. It ached, but it wasn't unbearable. He could do this. He banged his shield against his breastplate and something odd caught his gaze.

His breastplate was dented and cracked right where Destrian had rammed his lance. Just how hard did Destrian hit him? None of the other knights had even left a scratch.

From the other side of the list, Destrian, his visor up, flashed him a cruel smile. He seemed untouched, even though Alistair had splintered at least one lance off him.

Alistair scowled with all the hate in his heart. This time he was going to get him. This time the crown would be his.

The herald slashed the flag in a downward arc and the third course began.

Alistair kicked Snapper into a gallop. "Hyah!"

As he closed in on Destrian, he lowered his lance and pointed it at his target. He poured all his focus on that one spot between shoulder and breast. His injury blazed again, but he suffered through the pain, gritting his teeth and gripping the lance so hard his hand began to hurt.

The lances made an explosive contact, so explosive that Alistair's breastplate shattered like glass.

He flew off the saddle and crashed on the ground, tumbling before stopping completely, his arms and legs spread-eagled.

He gasped for air, each inhalation sending a crushing pain through his chest and lungs.

And all around him the crowd cheered Destrian's name.

#

Leera had no more tears left. Her dry eyes were strained. She held her father's stiff hand in hers. Already his warmth had fled. He was still. Impossibly still.

Feet shuffled behind her. Her mother stood, flanked by several guards. The color drained from Ursula's face as the situation before her took root. Her husband was dead. She opened her mouth as if to say something but no words came out.

Her expression grew sad and tears misted her eyes. A small piece of Leera was glad to see it because it meant that Ursula did love her father, even if she'd been forced to marry him.

"The king is dead," a guard said.

As one the other guards said, "Long live the king."

Long live the king? Then it struck her. "The tournament." She brushed her hair behind her ears. "Has a victor been announced?"

Ursula's eyes registered her daughter for the first time since she'd entered the room. She nodded slowly, swallowed, then licked her lips. "Rowanark's new king is Sir Destrian."

He lost. Her Alistair had lost.

Her whole life was about to change.

Chapter Seventeen

Alistair hissed as he undid the bandage that was wrapped around his torso. Good, there was hardly any blood. Not as bad as it had been three days ago, when he'd reopened it and only made things worse for him. Since then, he'd been confined to bed, sleeping mostly. Anything was better than dealing with reality.

Anything was better than dealing with his loss.

A maid came to his door, saw him without a shirt on, and bowed her head. He should've closed his door instead of standing around shirtless. Quickly, Alistair covered his wound with a fresh bandage and slipped on his tunic. He picked up the old bandage from the floor and stuffed it in the pot with the rest of them, then passed the pot to the maid.

"There's less blood on these," he said. "Thank you for taking care of me."

She remained standing, her hands clasped in front of her. Alistair narrowed his eyes, scrutinizing her. It wasn't the same maid that came in to bring him fresh bandages or water. That one had dark hair where this one had blond.

The maid lifted her head.

Leera.

"Hi," she said. Or rather breathed. Something behind her tone niggled at Alistair. She sounded…frightened.

But why?

A storm of emotions ran through Alistair. How should he feel? Happy that she was there? Sad that this would probably be their last moment together? Ashamed? Angry? Remorseful?

Her eyes were swollen, as if she'd been crying. Of course, she had. She had every right to cry and no one could hold it against her.

"I'm sorry," Alistair said, "about your father."

"Thank you. Will you be at the ceremony?"

Alistair lowered his gaze. "I don't know."

"I see."

The ceremony to honour her father would lead into her marriage, and he definitely didn't want to be in Rowan for that. The farther he was from the wedding, the better.

Anger. That was the emotion he chose. Or rather chose him.

"Why are you here?" he said, in a sharp tone he wished he could take back. Great—now she'd think he was upset with her.

"I've…" she paused, as if debating what words to use and Alistair braced himself, "come to say goodbye."

That struck him harder than any lance could.

"So you're going to go through with the wedding?"

"I don't have a choice."

"Yes, you do." He looked up at her. Was she giving up? "You always had a choice."

"And what is that?"

"Run away with me." He held her hands, drawing them together and to his chest. "We'll leave Rowanark."

"Where would we go?"

"Anywhere but here. There are other cities, towns. Other kingdoms." He'd only been as far as Teerdock, but there was more to the world than just Rowanark. "Ours is not the only kingdom."

They could start a new life together. Forget titles or duty. Surely that sounded better than any life they were heading into now.

She fell into him and he hugged her close. She was small and fragile in his arms. His senses were hyper aware of her touch. He never wanted to let her go.

"I can't."

"Please, Leera. We can start our own life together."

"I can't leave."

"Why not?"

"I can't leave behind everything my father built. I'm Princess of Rowanark. My place is here. I belong here. It's my duty." She pulled back from him. "No, I don't care about my duty. I'm doing this for my father. Please understand. I have to do this."

Truth was, he did understand. The love she had for her father was boundless, unconditional, and unmatched. Despite what King Hayden had done to Reynard and Ursula, he had been a good father. He couldn't just steal away the princess. He was the one that lost the tournament. He shouldn't expect her to turn away from her father, from her people, from the life she was destined to lead.

Yet in her eyes, her resolve began to crumble. If he asked one more time, she would cave in and go with him.

But he spared her and didn't ask again.

Instead, he kissed her lips softly.

"He'll never kiss better than me," he said.

"Then you'd better kiss me some more."

He did. Every kiss was slow, deliberate. He had to remember the way her lips felt against his, the way she tasted, the way she seemed to fit perfectly in his arms.

When he stopped kissing her, he laid his cheek on hers. "I don't want to let you go."

"I know."

"I love you."

"I love you. Always."

He kissed her again. He couldn't stop. He wouldn't stop.

She was the one who pulled back from him. She was the one who backed away. She was much stronger than him. She knew they couldn't be in this room together forever. That at one point or another, he would go back to Teerdock and she would marry Destrian and be Queen of Rowanark.

Without a final goodbye, she turned from him and was gone.

#

Leera didn't get far.

She pushed her back against the wall next to Alistair's door and the tears burst from her eyes. An ache formed in her chest and pulsed with each heart beat. She was breaking. That was the only way to describe it. Saying goodbye to her father was hard enough, but saying goodbye to Alistair was like saying goodbye to a future she had wanted but wouldn't have.

She took a shuddering breath. No sounds came from Alistair's room. He must have been standing there, stunned.

Down the hall, Reynard leaned against the wall with his arms crossed. He raised a finger to his mouth.

How long had he been standing there? Judging by the hollowed look on his face, he'd heard everything and it had affected him somehow. No doubt it would have, for he'd gone through the exact same thing with Ursula.

At last, she understood her mother. Ursula had had to let Reynard go as Leera had let Alistair go. Her mother had been trying to protect her this whole time by pushing Destrian onto her. It wasn't that she liked Destrian—not at all—but that she knew Destrian would win the tournament and wanted to make certain Leera wasn't attached to anyone else.

This whole time her mother had been looking out for her; had not wanted her to live through the heartache she had.

It's too late, Mother.

A big crash sounded from Alistair's room, followed by another and then another. Leera jerked. She closed a fist over her heart. Her Alistair was in pain, and she had been the cause of it.

She looked at Reynard and with her eyes conveyed her first order as future queen.

Take care of him.

He nodded, seeming to understand.

#

Alistair lifted the chair over his head and shattered it against the stone floor. It splintered, and he tossed the remains.

That felt better.

But it wasn't enough. Rage tore through him. He picked up another chair and threw it against the wall. So what if he caused a mess? So what if this didn't change his fate?

He grabbed his travel bag and hauled it on the bed. From the chest, he pulled out his clothes and stuffed them in the bag.

"Going somewhere?" Reynard. He stood by the doorway, arms crossed over his chest. Alistair sneered at him. Reynard had thought him unworthy to be king or of Leera's love. He'd forbade him from seeing her and now any chance Alistair had of seeing Leera again was gone.

"Back to Teerdock," Alistair said. "There's nothing here for me anymore."

"You can't leave yet."

"You expect me to stick around for the wedding?" Losing the tournament was bad enough. Sticking around for the wedding would be like adding salt to a wound.

"You're giving up on her?"

Alistair stopped packing. "The tournament's over. What more can I do?"

What was Reynard trying to get at? Alistair wasn't giving up on Leera. Rather, his options had run out. Surely, Reynard could see that.

"You can still fight for her."

He had, and lost. What game was Reynard playing?

"It's done, Reynard." He crammed the last of his clothes in the bag, tied the knot and shouldered the load. His wound stung, but it was a lot better than it had been. "She said so herself."

Leera had accepted her fate. Now he had to accept his own and move on, ignoring every fibre of his being screaming at him to do exactly what Reynard told him to do now.

Fight on.

But fight what? That was the problem. He had no answer and neither, it seemed, did Reynard. He pushed past him to the hallway and down to the stairs.

Reynard followed him. "You're just going to run away?"

"Yup."

"Not even going to try?"

"I did," Alistair said, hopping down the steps. "I failed. Time to go back to my old life."

"Old life? Is that really what you want?"

No, it wasn't, but it was the only life he had left. His father wouldn't even be disappointed. In a strange twist, his father would probably be proud that he'd made it that far in the tournament. And now everyone in Rowanark knew where Teerdock was, that it was more than just a backwater fiefdom. He'd put Teerdock on the map. He'd even proven himself better than most of the knights. Those were achievements to be proud of, right?

They were. But he wanted more. He'd wanted to prove himself as Destrian's better. He wanted Leera. He'd accomplished much, but not what he'd wanted for himself.

"There's nothing more I can do," Alistair said as he bounded outside and made a straight line toward the castle gates. Gray clouds formed above, and the air was heavier than normal. Hopefully those clouds would stick around and it would rain on Destrian's wedding day. But by Cosima, even that was out of his control. "Nothing either of us can do. Not me. Not Leera. Our paths crossed for a moment, but whatever we had is over now."

"Don't do what I did."

Alistair stopped cold. It wasn't what Reynard had said, but how he'd said it. It sounded like a warning. No, like a plea.

"I should've done everything in my power to stop King Hayden from marrying the woman I loved. She was mine and I was hers. But I didn't stop him. I let him have her. I gave up, just like you're doing now. It was the worst mistake I've ever made."

"He's king now." Alistair's back was toward Reynard. "Destrian is king. What do you expect me to do? Raise an army and take over the kingdom? Be the next Black Knight?"

Wouldn't that be something? It almost sounded like a good idea. Almost.

"I expect you to act like a knight."

Alistair spun around. "I am! For once I'm doing what you want me to do. I'm respecting Leera's wish and honouring the tournament."

Honour and duty. Wasn't that a knight? What more did Reynard want from him?

"Your father didn't raise a coward." In his hand, Reynard held Alistair's sword, the one he'd given him when he'd knighted Alistair. Alistair must've forgotten it in his room as he hurried out. "And I sure as the Great Depths didn't tutor one." His expression hardened. "I thought you came here to prove to everyone you were worthy of your knighthood and of the crown."

"I am, damn it."

Reynard shoved the sword to his chest. "Then prove it."

Soon after, they both stood across from each other at the list, each holding their own sword.

"If I beat you in a duel," Alistair said, "you'll let me leave?"

"If you beat me in a duel I'll let you make the biggest mistake of your life and yes, leave."

"This is ridiculous." Alistair gripped the handle on his sword. He'd had this sword for years but only ever used it a handful of times. He had a natural talent with the sword, though. He slashed the air and tested its weight.

"Scared?" Reynard twirled his own sword.

"You wish."

"You've never beaten me before."

"Maybe when I was a squire."

"Let's see if you've improved then."

Gladly. Alistair surged toward him and swung his sword overhead. Reynard blocked the attack and countered. Alistair jumped back then lunged forward, and Reynard parried the blade aside.

"You're going to have to do better than that," Reynard said.

"I'm just warming up."

Alistair pressed his attack fast and hard. He forced Reynard on the defensive.

"Does the scenery bother you?" Reynard said as he blocked each blow with efficiency.

"Should it?"

"It's where you lost everything."

"It's where I won, too."

Sparks flew each time their blades met.

"Those matches don't count," Reynard said. "The only one that mattered was the one against Destrian."

Reynard parried then countered, swiping his sword. Alistair leapt back, the blade missing him by a hair's breadth.

Reynard advanced. "A knight doesn't run away."

Right now, Alistair couldn't care less. His breathing grew rapid, the sword heavier in his grasp. He'd put everything he'd had in his last series of attacks and it had tired him. He rolled his shoulders then stabbed with his sword, feinted, and stabbed again.

His blade hit metal. Damn, Reynard was a lot better than Alistair remembered. Had he been toying with Alistair all the times they'd trained before?

Now it was Reynard's turn to press his own attack as his sword swept down at Alistair. Each blow Alistair parried left his arm shaky and numb.

"A knight is honourable," Reynard said. "Strong. Determined."

"I know all that," Alistair said through clenched jaw, more focused on staying alive than pondering the Knight's Code.

With two hands Reynard lifted his sword up and swung it in a downward arc. Alistair raised his sword with both hands and blocked the devastating blow. Reynard leaned his weight into his sword. Alistair resisted, his arms trembling.

"But did you know a knight is about servitude?" Reynard was calm, and didn't look the least bit worn out. "It's not about what he wants. A knight isn't selfish. A knight is there for the kingdom. He's no greater than the farmer. No, in fact, he's less than a farmer. No one is above him, and yet he's the only one who can help the people of Rowanark. He's a servant to the people. Just like a king."

The truth of that burned in Alistair. Had he led his life as a knight of servitude? Maybe he hadn't. Maybe all those times he'd helped the

Teerdock farmers wasn't about them at all, but about himself. He'd wanted to be liked.

He shook his head. "Just shut up and fight!"

Reynard pushed even harder and brought Alistair down to one knee. "Worthiness isn't about proving you're better than someone else. It's about proving that you can make other lives better. It's putting someone else's needs ahead of your own. It's sacrifice. You think you can do that? You think you can put the people of Rowanark ahead of your own selfish needs? You think you can do that for Leera?"

"Yes!" Alistair spat.

"Then prove it!"

With all his strength, and a battle cry so loud all of Rowanark could hear him, Alistair drove Reynard's sword back, and Reynard retreated several paces. Alistair advanced harder and faster until he got close enough that he gripped Reynard's wrist and twisted his sword around. He was about to disarm Reynard and take his sword, when, instead, Reynard dropped the sword of his own volition and kicked at Alistair's stomach, but he still held onto Reynard and sidestepped, pulling Reynard across where he'd been standing.

Alistair charged after him, sword raised. He wasn't going to kill Reynard, but he would make him yield.

Reynard's back was to him. Alistair swung his sword down.

Reynard spun around. A blue light flashed and Alistair's sword clanged against it.

Clanged? Against light?

He couldn't see what it was. The light was too bright. Reynard kicked him and he fell back hard on the mud.

The light faded and Reynard stood having retrieved his sword. The corner of his lip curved up.

"I had you," Alistair said.

"I haven't yielded."

Alistair narrowed his eyes. What was that light? He'd never seen anything like it. Was it a trick? A powder that exploded in light when released into the air?

No. Reynard wasn't one for theatrics.

Then what? What had it been?

It reminded him of…the Twelve Knights of Old. It was said they had blades of light that they could summon at a moment's notice.

The gray skies above moved, and the sun's bright light winked for a moment before it was clouded once more.

So that had been it. And as for what his sword had hit against, it had probably been a dagger Reynard had hidden on his person.

Ha! As if Reynard was one of the Twelve Knights. They'd been dead for hundreds of years.

"Giving up?" Reynard tapped the blade of his sword—his real, steel sword—against his shoulder.

Swiftly, Alistair jumped up and charged after Reynard. His sword lashed out, and Reynard, instead of jumping back, blocked the attack, stepped closer to Alistair, gripped Alistair's sword arm, then swept a foot across Alistair's legs, tripping him.

Again, Alistair fell to the ground face first, the wet mud splashing in his face. Before he could get up, Reynard kicked him down with his boot, then slammed his sword right next to Alistair's ear. The sharp hissing split into Alistair's eardrum.

"And more than anything," Reynard said, "a knight never gives up. Not on his fiefdom. Not on his people. And not on the love of his life. I tried to teach you that, but I couldn't because I'm not a knight either." He tugged his sword from the ground and tossed it aside. He lifted his foot off Alistair's chest. "Go home, Alistair. You're right. There's nothing more for us here."

Reynard walked away. Alistair groaned and turned on his side. Reynard had beaten him easily.

There's nothing more for us here. That wasn't true. Everything was here in Rowan. Everything he wanted ever since he was a page. Yes, he'd resisted that when he'd been bullied by the other pages, and that had sullied the majesty of Rowan, but deep down, he still wanted it.

He pounded a fist on the ground and something stabbed him. Blood oozed from a small cut. Whatever he'd touched was sharp enough to draw blood.

Running his hand over the spot, he searched for it and touched something hard. Not a rock. This was different. He picked it up and rolled it over in his palm.

A piece of metal. A sharp piece of metal. He surveyed the ground and found more pieces. Some were bigger than others. It was hard and burnished, like iron. Did it come from his shattered breastplate?

No. It was almost black. So where did it come from?

The lances? No, they were made of wood.

Or should've been.

"Reynard!" Alistair called, getting up.

Reynard stopped and turned to him. Alistair showed him his discovery. Reynard narrowed his eyes at the piece of iron.

Alistair smiled. "Does a knight cheat?"

Chapter Eighteen

Alistair stood in the back with Reynard at his side watching as, one by one, people approached the gold-encrusted casket to say their goodbyes. Many shed tears. Queen Ursula sat in a chair and accepted the condolences with a steady nod. She didn't cry but kept her regal countenance firmly in place. She had to be a pillar for the kingdom.

Leera stood above the casket. She kept her face stoic, her lips a rigid line. How much was she keeping back? She had a vacant look in her eyes, staring down at the body of her father lying in a casket, his eyes closed, never to be opened again. Destrian stood next to her, his hand on her back.

The priest said a few words, bestowing his blessings on the deceased and those he had left behind. Much of the nobility attended, but there were still a few missing. Alistair's father was one. Not that he wouldn't have wanted to be there, but the trip from Teerdock to Rowan was a few days. It would've taken too long.

Following the ceremony, the casket was closed and King Hayden was led out to be buried.

The next day was Leera's wedding.

She was white as the sun blazing high on a summer sky. Her flowing white dress heightened her beauty to a level Alistair had never witnessed before. She was perfect. Angelic, even. Her expression didn't match, though. This was her wedding day, and yet she had the face of one walking to her execution.

Destrian was with her, a smug, pompous look on his face. How Alistair hated that look. He should be in awe of the woman standing next to him, not using her to elevate his own stature. He didn't appreciate her. He didn't deserve her.

And Alistair could prove it.

He waited, biding his time as he listened to the priest conduct the ceremony. He hadn't been to many weddings himself. It sounded beautiful, as if the priest made into words what Alistair felt in his heart for Leera.

Then his moment arrived.

"Does anyone here," the priest said, "wish to state a claim why these two should not be joined as husband and wife?"

Silence. Leera gave Alistair a fleeting glance before her gaze dropped to the floor. Destrian stared point blank at him, almost daring him to say something. Even some of the other knights, nobles, and people of Rowanark turned their heads to see if Alistair would speak out.

But he kept his mouth as a thin line. He couldn't smile either. That would give him away.

Everyone turned back to the front.

The priest surveyed the crowd, and nodded. "Then by the power and glory and grace of the Lady Cosima—"

Alistair raised his hand. "Wait a moment," he said, jumping up from his seat. "There's a few things I'd like to say before the Lady Cosima binds these two together."

Murmurings rumbled through the chapel. Alistair picked up bits and pieces of it. Something about how he was going to get himself thrown in jail or worse. That he'd lost his mind.

"Give it up, Alistair," Destrian said. "You lost. Go back to your farm in Teerdock."

Alistair smirked at the remark but refused to let it get to him. He was in control now, everyone had their eyes and ears open to him. "I did. But did I lose fairly?"

Destrian narrowed his eyes.

Leera opened her mouth to speak but her mother beat her to it.

"What are you suggesting, Sir Alistair?" Queen Ursula asked.

"Nothing," Destrian said, snarling. "He's just trying to delay the inevitable. Face it, Alistair. You're a sore loser." He put an arm around Leera and pulled her to him. "How dare you address your future king this way?"

Ursula lifted a hand and quieted him. "You have not been crowned yet." She gave Alistair an inquisitive stare. He couldn't tell whose side she was on. Maybe her curiosity was sparked? That worked, as long as she was willing to listen to him. "And be aware that if your claim is unfounded, you could very well be thrown in prison for your interference in this royal affair."

Alistair bowed. "I know, Your Highness. But to stay silent would be to accept the fact that Destrian cheated the tournament rules, the Kingdom of Rowanark, and, more than anything, cheated your daughter."

An audible gasp sounded. Ursula lifted a hand once more and demanded silence.

"Can you prove this?" she asked.

Leera broke from Destrian and stepped forward. Hope glimmered in her eyes and Alistair nodded to her.

"I can," Alistair said.

"How?"

Destrian paled, his fingers curled into tight fists by his side.

"With this." Alistair brandished the iron fragment.

Ursula frowned. "And what is that?"

"It's a piece of iron from a broken lance." Alistair turned to the people, showing the evidence. "This was what smashed into my armor. I always thought my armor was impenetrable." He turned back to the queen. "And it is, against wood or even a swipe from a hammer. But when you have a pointed lance coming at you at a horse's full gallop, the force of the blow is that much stronger. Strong enough, in fact, to shatter one's breastplate."

Ursula shook her head. "That's not possible. Our lances are made of wood."

"I thought so, too." Alistair stuffed the iron piece in his pocket and pulled out a book. "That's what the rule book on jousting says, at least. Let's see." He flipped through the pages, and stopped at the spot he wanted. "The manual states that tournament jousts are friendly matches meant to test the technique and accuracy of a knight and that serious injury should be avoided at all cost. To limit injuries, the head of lances will be made of hollow wood, which would splinter when contacting an opponent's shield or breastplate." He snapped the book shut. "I have reason to believe that Sir Destrian wasn't using lances made of hollow wood."

"Nonsense," Destrian blurted out. "You can't prove it. What? Because you have a piece of iron that you think came from *my* lance?" He blew air between his cheeks, which sounded less than kingly. "Please, Alistair. This is farfetched even for you. Who's to say that iron fragment isn't what's left of your breastplate?"

"I thought the same thing." Alistair tossed the rule book so it landed flat by Destrian's feet. "But the iron I found was nearly black." His confidence rose with each word he uttered. He was even enjoying this. "My breastplate was a light gray. Almost silver. I think you switched the lances."

"These are accusations," Destrian said, but he couldn't hide the beads of sweat forming on his forehead. "You have no proof."

"I don't?" Alistair crossed his arms and cocked an eyebrow.

"You're forgetting that we only went through three courses and used only three lances. You had one lance remaining."

Destrian's mouth opened. The color drained from his face. He was finished, and he knew it.

"And guess what? I have that lance."

The doors opened and Reynard came in carrying a lance. He brought it to the front.

"I had one of the squires in charge of the lances show it to me." He took the lance from Reynard and weighed it in his hands. "Hm. Feels a little heavy." He looked at Ursula. "You'll find, Your Highness, that under this wooden frame…" Reynard produced a hammer and smashed the tip of the lance, revealing a near black iron stump in the shape of a fist. "This is how Sir Destrian won the tournament. By cheating."

Shock reverberated through the crowd. Gasps, sighs and mutterings. A smile spread across Leera's mouth. Tears glistened in her eyes. Happy, hopeful tears.

Destrian's face reddened, his body shaking. "You can't deny that you lost."

"True enough. But the rules state that if any match is found to be in violation of the rules, then a rematch can be called."

Destrian sneered. "Yes, and the rules also state that the host of the tournament must decide whether a rematch is warranted. And that host is the king. Which is me."

The priest, Cosima bless him, cleared his throat. "You haven't taken the wedding vows yet, Sir Destrian."

Alistair smiled. "Then it falls to the princess."

"No," Ursula said, "it falls to the queen."

That didn't bode well. Alistair hadn't counted on that part. Destrian grinned like he'd have the last laugh. Leera's face clouded over; she'd told Alistair more than once how much Ursula loved

Destrian, that she wanted him to be king. But she couldn't ignore the facts, could she?

Maybe she could. She was queen. Ruler of Rowanark. She could decree whatever she damn well wanted.

Alistair swallowed, then held his breath.

Queen Ursula didn't look at Alistair or at Destrian. Her focus was on Reynard, and the two of them locked eyes. Something passed between them. Was she remembering the times she had with him? They had been engaged once, before the king had taken her for himself. She had loved Reynard, as Leera loved Alistair, and maybe she still did. Her expression softened, a smile curved her lips. It was the first time Alistair had ever seen her smile, a warm, hopeful smile.

She turned to her daughter and nodded. "The tournament's not over yet."

\#

"I'm sorry," Alistair said.

Sybil cocked an eyebrow at him, but kept her lips firmly pressed together. Her arms were folded over her chest and one leg crossed over the other. Alistair sat facing her in her house. After the way he had treated her at the castle gates, he counted himself lucky she'd even agreed to see him.

But seeing him and talking to him were two different things. Though he sat in a chair, he ought to be down on his knees begging for her forgiveness.

Behind her, Walter paced back and forth, shaking his head at Alistair.

"I was an idiot," Alistair said.

Walter snorted. "You can say that again."

"It was a stupid thing to do."

"And insensitive," Walter added.

Alistair nodded eagerly. "Definitely insensitive."

She must've been furious with him. Usually when Walter interrupted, she always told him to shut up and butt out of it. Not this time. She let Walter spew his nonsense like he was her ambassador. Reynard stood next to Alistair. He had his arms crossed over his chest same as his sister. Had the same look on his face as Sybil, too, but where Sybil was angry, Reynard was confused.

"I started drinking again because of it," Walter said.

"You have?" Alistair asked. Walter had done so well in his sobriety, and it had been, in part, thanks to Alistair. But it meant nothing if Alistair was also the reason Walter went back to the bottle.

Walter stopped and gave a sheepish smile. "Not really. I rather like being sober." He quickly shot Alistair a glare and jabbed a finger at him. "How dare you speak to my wife like that? You ought to be ashamed."

"I am," Alistair said. "I know I don't deserve your help, but I need it. You're the only one who can help me."

Truthfully, any blacksmith would've loved to make a fresh piece of plated armor for him. But Sybil's work was unrivaled, and this match would be the fight of his life. He only wanted the best. Another's handiwork would not do.

"Damn right," Walter said. "She's the only one who can help any of—"

"Why?"

The word cut through Walter's yammering even though Sybil had whispered it. Alistair's concentration was all on Sybil. Alistair would've heard her in a hail storm.

Still, what did she mean?

She must've read the perplexed look on his face because she continued.

"Why did you treat me that way?"

"How did you treat my sister?" Reynard said, his tone honed with brotherly protectiveness. He'd never referred to Sybil as his sister before. Not so explicitly, at least, and not in front of her.

"Like dirt," Walter said. "Worse than I ever treated her and I raised my hand to her."

"Shut up, Walter."

That Walter raised his hand to Sybil was true—Alistair had seen it himself—but he doubted severely that he'd ever hit her. The more he'd gotten to know them both, the more apparent it became who wore the trousers and who the homespun dress.

"Tell my brother," Sybil said.

He could, but Reynard wasn't going to like it. But Sybil wanted Alistair to confess. His stomach knotted.

"She had come to the castle and the guards wouldn't let her through." Alistair dipped his head. No matter how many times he'd seen Reynard's disappointing stare, it never got any easier. "I could've ordered them to stand down and let her pass. They would've listened to me. But I didn't. I let them keep her out and I…" He swallowed. This was the hardest part. "I turned my back on her."

Alistair steeled himself. *Here it comes…*

Reynard took in a loud breath from his nose as if preparing himself for a tirade. "You arrogant—"

"I know," Alistair said. "I'm arrogant and all I care about is myself." He could reprimand himself as Reynard word for word. "That's why I did it. Because for the first time in my life the knights treated me like their equal. I didn't want to spoil that. But it was wrong. Who cares what the knights would've thought? My behavior was shameful. Reprehensible. It's not how a knight should act. I'm sorry. I just wanted to be liked."

Cosima, that sounded pathetic.

Shame twisted inside him like a dagger. Who knew baring his soul and all its inner hurts would be that hard? For a split second, Sybil's expression softened. And then she caught herself and her eyes narrowed darkly.

Reynard sighed. "I'm sorry, too."

What? Even Sybil looked surprised by this turn of events.

"I abandoned you, sister, when you needed me most. Don't blame, Alistair. I taught him, but I, too, had much still to learn. If I could go back in time, I never would've left without a word. I would've come to you. I would've pleaded with the king that my soiled reputation shouldn't tarnish my family's. But I didn't do that. I was too concerned with myself to care, and that carried through to my squire. I'm sorry, Sybil. We're sorry." Reynard bowed his head. "Please, give me another chance to prove to you that I'm a good brother."

Sybil stood up. Walter braced himself for the onslaught, as did Alistair.

Then the most bizarre thing happened. Sybil's eyes watered and a tear rolled down her cheek. She cupped Reynard's cheek and forced him to look at her. She gave the slightest smile before embracing him. Reynard closed his arms around his sister.

Walter's jaw hung open, awe-struck. "I swear, in all the years I've been married to her I've never seen her cry."

She burst out a chuckle. "Shut up, Walter."

"Yes, dear."

"Will you help me?" Alistair said.

Sybil pulled away from Reynard, but he left his arm around her shoulder and she left hers around his waist. Standing side by side, they could've been identical twins.

"You need new armor?" she said.

"I do."

She winked. "I have just the thing."

Chapter Nineteen

The crowds didn't cheer. Though the terraces were bursting, they didn't call out to Alistair or Destrian. They sat and waited and watched. The intensity in the air was almost palpable.

"It's so quiet," Alistair said at his end of the list. He shivered against the cold. The temperature had fallen the past couple of days, and the cool chainmail under Sybil's new plate armor wasn't helping.

"The people were cheated of a king," Konrad said. "They don't know who or what to believe anymore."

"They've lost their faith in the royal family."

Konrad rolled his eyes. "What royal family?"

A princess who couldn't rule on her own and a queen who had been in love with someone other than the king. A royal family, sure, but a dysfunctional one.

"Your father is here," Reynard said.

"He is?" Alistair scanned the crowd. Pydor must've gotten word about the king's passing and traveled to the castle as quickly as he could. Little did he know that he'd be treated to a jousting match featuring his own son as a finalist.

"He came to see you, but you were preoccupied."

Alistair nodded. He hadn't talked to a single soul all day. Konrad had helped him put on his armor in silence. Like the armor before it, this suit that Sybil crafted was as light as silk and as hard as a castle's fortifications. She claimed it was the strongest armor she'd ever made and wouldn't break even if Destrian used iron again. The armor looked and felt the same as the one Sybil had made before it, but something was different. As strange as it sounded, the armor seemed to sparkle. Not everywhere and not blindingly, but here and there was a shine to the armor that was more than simple polish. When Alistair investigated the breastplate further he saw small crystals embedded in the breastplate, and when he'd asked Sybil about it, she told him she'd want him to look like one of the Twelve Knights of Old. It was said their armor, too, was made of brilliant crystal and diamond, and shining jewels.

"Did you talk to him?" Alistair asked.

"He says he's very proud of you."

Alistair spotted his father sitting among the people of Rowanark. He looked a little out of place compared to the crowd in a colorful tunic. Pydor lifted his hand and waved, a big smile donning his face.

"He always was." Even if Alistair had lost in the first round of the tournament, his father still would've been proud of him. The same couldn't have been said for Reynard.

On the other side of the list, Destrian paced back and forth, his gauntleted hands in tight fists and his arms swinging violently. He looked like a wolf getting ready to pounce on its prey. Though his expression was a mask of fury, he was focused. His eyes were trained on Alistair. His bearing left a seedling of doubt in the pit of Alistair's stomach. As much as Destrian didn't like Alistair, he'd never been this incensed with him. He'd always come off as if he were above Alistair. Now the two of them were equal, and it was obvious he didn't like that at all.

"Your horse, Sir Alistair," said a squire, offering the reins to him.

"Thank you." Alistair rubbed underneath Snapper's jaw. "All

right, buddy, so I lied to you. *This* is now the last time we ride together. Then you can go back to Leera. I promise."

Snapper made a sound. Not quite a snort. Almost like a grunt.

"Do you think we can win?"

As if Snapper could understand him, he reared up on his hind legs and kicked out, whinnying so loudly it shocked the crowd.

"All right, all right." Alistair laughed. "You're a good horse. I have half a mind to keep you for myself when I'm king." Snapper bared his teeth. "All right, fine. I'll get a different horse."

Snapper nudged his muzzle against Alistair's breastplate. Alistair put his arms around the horse. It was an awkward embrace, but an embrace nonetheless.

"Help me win. Please."

He placed a foot on the stirrup and climbed up on the saddle.

"Good luck out there," Konrad said.

"Thanks, Konrad, for everything. You were a good teacher."

"And you a good student. Nothing can stop you now from getting what you want." Konrad smirked.

"What's so funny?"

"I find it odd that the man who taught the next king of Rowanark used to be a general in the Black Knight's army."

"You didn't teach him everything he knows," Reynard said, a lance in his hand.

Konrad shrugged. "Fair enough." Before backing off, he gave Alistair a wink.

Reynard passed the lance to Alistair. "Do what you need to do."

Alistair nodded and took the lance, feeling its weight. The lances had been newly prepared by the craftsmen in the castle to ensure no further tampering.

Before shutting the visor on his helmet, he glanced over at the royal terrace. Instead of sitting, Leera stood by the balustrade, watching him. She smiled when his eyes caught hers. It was a tranquil, confident smile.

This was different from his last match with Destrian. Then, he'd been angry and desperate and, worse, in pain from a fresh injury. Now he was recovered, well rested, and assured of his success. Nothing gave Destrian a leg up this time. It was a fair fight. And sure, the crowds weren't cheering and roaring as they usually did, but that lent itself to a serene atmosphere, not a disquieting one.

The herald raised the flag and slashed it down and the match began.

Alistair kicked Snapper and they charged down the list at an incredible speed. Destrian's horse reared up, made a terrifying sound, then tore down the list. Alistair focused on his target, Destrian's breastplate. He didn't blink, and his breaths came in slow and fulsome, in through his nostrils and out through his mouth.

He had to be calm and sturdy. Unwavering and solid. His grip tightened around the lance's handle as he lowered its tip. He had utter control, as if the lance were an extension of his arm.

He aimed and jabbed the lance, hitting Destrian's breastplate.

At the same time, Destrian's lance splintered off his own breastplate and he tensed every part of his body, resisting the impact.

Now the crowd roared; they couldn't help it. They cheered and applauded and whistled and shouted. It was like they'd risen from a deep slumber and were happy to be alive. Their clamor filled the inner list.

"Did you feel anything?" Reynard asked.

"Not a thing," Alistair said. "Sybil's armor is as good as ever."

"At least this time we know he isn't cheating," Konrad said, and gave Alistair his second lance.

The second course began. The muscles around Alistair's mouth tightened and his lips curved up. He smiled, enjoying the joust. Even with everything riding on this match, he couldn't deny he was truly having fun.

He aimed the lance for Destrian's chest, but before he made contact, Destrian knocked his lance with the edge of his shield. The lance hit, but didn't splinter, so it didn't count as a point. As for Destrian, he missed, puncturing air.

It was a strange move. A coward's move. He must've been afraid.

Either that, or he wanted Alistair to waste a lance. They only had two left and they were tied in points, one for each.

"What a cheap trick." Alistair lifted his visor and spat. Was it fear or strategy that motivated Destrian?

"Don't let it get to you," Reynard said.

"Reynard's right. Destrian blocked it because he's afraid. Don't forget that."

Alistair nodded. He looked to Leera. Her beaming, encouraging smile was still etched on her face. Maybe he read into Destrian's motives too much. Konrad was right—fear moved Destrian, not strategy.

The third course began. Snapper darted down the list and Alistair tucked the lance under his armpit and levelled it at Destrian. In seconds, the horses closed the gap between them and—

Destrian's lance broke off Alistair's breastplate, hitting him right in the upper corner. The force of the blow knocked Alistair's aim and his lance missed its target. Worse, Alistair teetered too far. He dropped his shield, tossed the lance, and gripped the saddle. He'd been on the verge of falling but caught his balance just in time.

Alistair looked behind him at Destrian. He swooped his helmet off and raised a triumphant fist in the air, yelling out a battle cry. He grinned with all his teeth at Alistair. He didn't look the dandy that he had before. He looked like a fierce warrior.

He was an exceptional jouster, and admitting that left a cold lump in the pit of Alistair's stomach. The seed of doubt grew, and he clenched his jaw.

A squire had picked up his shield and handed it to him.

"You all right?" Reynard asked.

"He got me good." Alistair took the shield with a trembling hand. "I almost fell there."

"You're lucky you didn't."

Alistair took a breath. "He's better than I thought."

"He made it this far," Reynard said. "You thought he cheated the whole way?"

Alistair shrugged. "Was sort of hoping."

"You're better," Konrad said. "You can beat him."

"Can I?"

Wherever his confidence had gone, he needed it back. The weight of his match came crashing down on him. So much for thinking this would be an easy win. Of course, Destrian hadn't cheated the whole tournament. He was a seasoned jouster, had trained more than Alistair had. Alistair had some talent and Konrad had taught him well, but was it enough to win?

"Princess," Reynard said, and bowed.

"What?" Alistair whirled around in the saddle.

There she was, his Leera. And she wasn't in disguise either.

He swung down from Snapper and went to her, reaching out and grabbing her hands in his.

"What are you doing here?" he asked.

"I wanted to be here with you," she said. "I wanted to see you before your last course."

"I'm so glad you're here."

"You're shaking."

"I'm scared," he said, and it wasn't as difficult and embarrassing to admit to her as he thought it'd be.

"Don't be."

"But if I lose…"

She ran a hand over his cheek. "I'm here now. I'm not in disguise, either. I came as the Princess of Rowanark, as Leera. I wanted everyone to see me here and now with the man I love. The man I chose to love, not the man who was chosen for me. All this time I thought being a princess meant I had to follow a path laid out for me. But you showed me differently. You gave me a reason to choose my own path for myself. I think that was what my father wanted all along. It just took finding that one person worth living for. That's why he wanted this tournament. Not only to find the next King of Rowanark, but so that I could find the love of my life."

Alistair had been that person. But he couldn't just be her lover. If he was going to be with Leera, he had to be a lot more. "But am I worthy to call myself a knight? To become king? To be your husband?"

"You made it this far, haven't you?"

Her smile soothed him, eased his trembling. Cosima, was he ever glad for her presence. And she was right—he had come a long way. No ordinary knight could lose his horse and armor only to train with a new horse, be fitted to new armor, and beat the knights of Rowanark, and now joust one final time for the crown. Only a knight fit to be a king. He'd gone this far, and he had only a little bit more to go.

"I can't believe I've made it this far," he said. "No one thought I could, least of all myself. I came here out of spite, but I never thought it would truly be for me. Because I didn't think I was a knight. I didn't think I fit in with the rest of the knights, even if I was born a noble. I think I hated myself. I think I hated the life I was living because it wasn't much of one. Just wasted potential." He pulled her hand to his lips and kissed her delicate knuckle. "Until I saw you again. Until I started fighting for you. Until I saw that these knights weren't any worthier of the crown than I was. And that was when I realized I wasn't just fighting for you or just for me. I was fighting for the people of Rownark. I was making certain they had a king they could depend on."

She looked at him with both love and support. It was the same way she'd looked at him when they'd snuck off to the dungeon. Except now everyone watched. Alistair and Leera were on full display. There was no hiding, no disguises, no lies. They stood in their own truth for all to witness and accept.

"Get back on that horse," she said, "and claim your crown. It belongs to you."

"Thank you, Leera. I needed this." He glanced at her lips. "I want to kiss you so badly."

"What's stopping you?"

"There are a lot of people watching."

In fact, the reason the last course hadn't started was because of the two of them.

"Good. Let them see how a true knight can kiss."

And he did. He showed them all. He kissed her and he made the kiss last. And all around them the crowd went ballistic. A cacophony of cheers and whistles bombarded them. It was the loudest the crowd had ever been.

"I'll see you soon." He tucked a loose strand of hair behind her ear. Before turning away from her, he kissed the tip of her nose. He climbed back up on Snapper. "All right, Snapper, you heard the lady. Let's claim that crown."

Snapper snorted, dipping his head as if in agreement.

"You know what to do," Konrad said, passing him his last lance in King Hayden's tournament.

"Hit him hard and knock his ass off his horse."

Konrad winked. "Best technique I ever taught you."

He backed away and Reynard came forward.

"Any final piece of advice?" Alistair asked, his hand on his visor ready to snap it down.

"No advice. I just want you to know that no matter what happens here today, I'm proud of you."

Alistair froze. That was the last thing he expected Reynard to say, and yet, wasn't it what Alistair had always wanted to hear? And Reynard had said it truthfully. He had no reason to lie. Kissing Leera had renewed his confidence, but hearing Reynard's words gave him certainty in the very marrow of his bones that there would be only one victor in this match and it would be him.

He lowered the visor on his helmet. The herald lifted the flag for the last time. All was quiet. Nothing but the sound of Alistair's own breathing inside his helm.

Then the herald slashed the flag in a downward arc and Snapper surged down the list. Snapper's hooves pounded the earth, shooting dirt and debris into the air, the sound reverberating in Alistair's eardrums. Adrenaline pumped through him. In seconds the gap between him and Destrian closed. He lowered his lance and took aim.

He poured all his strength and determination into his final strike. This was for his father, for Teerdock. For Konrad and Walter and Sybil. For Reynard. For the people of Rowanark. For Leera. And for that page from Teerdock, many years ago, who'd always known he'd been destined for this precise moment.

He roared and felt the pressure of Destrian's lance splinter off his shield, felt his own lance hammer into Destrian's breastplate and shatter, bits of wood flying in every direction.

He'd hit him with everything he had.

He spun Snapper around in time to witness Destrian crash to the ground with an audible thud. He'd fallen so hard his body bounced once and then was still.

The crowd went wild. Alistair could hardly believe it. He'd won. He'd actually won. He'd knocked Destrian off his horse. The crown was his.

By Cosima—he was King of Rowanark.

He tore off his helmet and hopped off Snapper. Leera ran down the list and he ran to meet her. They collided into each other and he held her tightly, so tightly he risked suffocating her. He eased his embrace and kissed her.

He didn't just kiss the girl he loved. He kissed his future wife.

And he wanted everyone to know it.

Chapter Twenty

Alistair kicked the door open. The door led to the king and queen's chamber, newly furnished.

"Here, here! The king has arrived!" he said.

Leera's light and merry laughter left a warm feeling in his stomach. He could hear that laugh every day of his life. He *would* hear that laugh every day of his life. He carried her in his arms, the hem of her white dress dangling to the floor.

"Easy now," she said, placing a hand on his chest. "I think you've had a little bit too much to drink tonight."

"As I should, to honour the day of my wedding and my beautiful queen." He swiped the door with his foot, shutting it.

"*Wife.* Your beautiful wife."

"And my beautiful, perfect, extravagant wife." With her still in his arms, he danced around the room, the music the band played in the great hall still ringing in his ears.

She giggled. "Are you going to put me down, my handsome husband?"

He wiggled his eyebrows at her. "Yes."

He tossed her onto the bed, and she let out a yelp and then giggled some more. She was loud and she could be as loud as she wanted to be. Both of them could be. They didn't have to hide, didn't have to pretend anymore. They were in love, married, and bonded together for life.

She sobered and he watched as she slid between the sheets, her body arching and her long blond hair spread across the bed. In the white dress, she looked like an angel with a golden halo. She was perfect. Everything he had ever wanted and more.

He couldn't wait to get in bed with her. He moved toward her to do just that.

She kicked her leg out, her foot resting on his chest and stopping his approach. "Will you miss home? Will you miss Teerdock?"

He paused. Did she have to ask him that *now*? The trousers he wore got noticeably tighter.

The serious look on her face meant she had to know. Was she worried that she had taken him away from a life he had lived for so long? Maybe she had. But she gave him a better life, a life they would share together.

Better life? More like the best life imaginable for a knight of noble birth. He was king! And still he could hardly believe it.

He kissed her toe and dropped her foot gently on the bed. "I'll miss seeing my father every day, and I'll miss drinking with the farmers." He might even miss the pig, Ollie. "But that's not my home. Not anymore. I don't quite have a home. I have to build one, a new one, with you. I hope you don't plan on trying to escape like you used to."

She raised an eyebrow, smiling seductively. "You think you'd catch me?"

Alistair smiled back. "Every time."

"My disguises are too good. You wouldn't be able to find me."

"No matter what disguise you wore, I always knew it was you."

Because he could see her for who she was. Not a princess, a maid, a guard, or a priestess. But Leera.

She ran a hand along the sheets. "Come to bed. Come lay with me."

His smile broadened. He must've looked ridiculous, but he couldn't help it.

"What's that smile for?" she asked.

"This."

And he jumped in, falling face first into bed with the love of his life.

Your Starter Library is Waiting for You!

It's important to me that I build a strong, close-knit relationship with my readers. It helps with my writing and lets me know what you'd like to see more of. I occasionally send updates with details on new releases, special offers and other exclusive, bonus content. By signing up, you'll be the first to know about everything related to the books, characters, and worlds I loved to create and I hope you love to read.

And if you sign up, I'll send you **two free books** to get your George Kayde library started. Those books are:

Table for Two – a romantic comedy set in Toronto about a sassy restauranteur and a savvy business consultant.

Knight in Training – a fantasy romance set in the Kingdom of Rowanark about a squire hellbent on becoming a knight and a village girl with a hidden past. This book also happens to be the prequel to the Rowanark Tournament series.

You get these two books **for free** by signing up at http://georgekayde.com/free-books/.

Enjoyed this book?
You can help make a difference!

If you've enjoyed this book, I would be forever grateful if you could spend just five minutes for a review (it can be as short as you like). Readers have more power than any publisher, publicist, or marketing firm. Thankfully, I have the best thing there is: **dedicated and loyal readers.**

Your honest review would make a difference because it helps bring my books to the attention of other readers.

Please leave review on the book's Amazon page.

Thanks very much. You rock my socks because you've taken the time to better my career and get more books to you in the future.

Acknowledgements

A huge thank you goes out to my editor, Nancy Cassidy, of Red Pen Coach. Her advice and stellar suggestions made this book the great, smooth read that it is today. I appreciated her eye to both the romantic elements and fantasy elements of this book.

I'd also like to thank Christa Holland of Paper and Sage Designs for the gorgeous cover, and Jennifer Litteken of the Killion Group for the fantastic book blurb.

I'd like to thank my wife, Catherine, for giving me the time, the space, and the support to write books. She's my super fan, and the first to hear all my story ideas. My parents, brother, goddaughter/sister-in-law (don't ask) and friends also deserve a shout-out for listening to me throughout the years go on and on about the writing.

And last, but definitely not least, I'd like to thank God. The Almighty always has my back.

About the Author

George Kayde lives in Toronto, Ontario, where he works his day job as a city planner for the City of Toronto. When he's not writing fiction or studying architectural plans, you can find him buried in a book, seated in the back row at the cinema or annoying his wife with improvised songs.

George writes love stories from the here and elsewhere. His stories take place in contemporary settings and in worlds dreamed up in his head. Regardless of where and when these stories take place, romance, love and relationships are always at the heart of them.

You can learn more about George Kayde in the following ways:
Website: www.georgekayde.com.
Facebook: https://www.facebook.com/georgekayde/
Twitter: @kaydegeorge.
Email: george@georgekayde.com.